Queen 517

Written by

Richard F. DeZerga

Cover Art By

Angelica Pasquali

ISBN: 1539184420
ISBN-13: 978-1539184423

DEDICATION

The writing process of this book was honestly so much fun. It would have been way less enjoyable and slower if it weren't for these lovely people:

Kathleen DeZerga, my mother who loved and supported me throughout the writing of my first book and this one.

Richard DeZerga, my father who I know is looking down on me from heaven and supporting me through every step of the way.

Joe Heap for helping me edit and name the book.

Alexa Schwalbe for her input, support, and popcorn.

CONTENTS

ACKNOWLEDGMENTS

I would like to thank everyone who supported me in any way big or small for my first book "The Mysterious Case of the Yellow County Lake". If you read it, critiqued it, posted about it on social media, or anything else I truly thank you. My Grandparents probably gave me the best criticism on that book, telling me things that I did well and things that I should change for the next time I write a book. One thing that they requested was to curse less. Well Grandma and Grandpa, I would like to apologize in advance.

CHAPTER 1

The rain cascaded onto the city street. It pounded so hard that the sound resembled cannon fire. Most people stayed inside on such a night. The people of this town were irritable and cranky. Anything could set them off, even a rain storm. Tonight was a torrential downpour. The streets and roads were collecting puddles around every street corner.

Inside a parking lot stood a police car. Within that police car, there were two officers.

"Blondie? Come on Sam you have to give me something other than that," Frank laughed. Officer Frank Stanley was a white man who stood about six feet high. Despite his young age of forty-three, his hair was all grey, even the hair on his mustache. His skin was wrinkly. Frank looked older than he really was.

"And so what if I like Blondie?" Samuel chuckled. He shoved a handful of French fries into his mouth.

"Sam, when I was a kid, we would beat up the fags who listened to Blondie," Frank continued.

"Bullshit, you are not that young. I know for a fact that Blondie didn't release anything until you were an adult. You are old Frank," Samuel spoke through a mouth full of fries. Samuel, a black man built like a truck, was well over six feet tall and had hands the size of dinner plates.

"Well I'm twenty-nine at heart," Frank smiled. He took a bite out of the burger in his lap.

"What about you? Who do you listen to?" Samuel asked while chomping.

"No one that I listen to is popular anymore," Frank answered.

"Oh, come on, just tell me. It's not like Blondie is popular anymore either," Samuel pressed.

"Alright fine. I love Santana," Frank answered.

"Oh yeah, Santana is long gone," Samuel laughed. "I haven't heard from them in years."

"Well you know what? I'm calling it. Santana will make a comeback soon," Frank predicted. Samuel laughed at him.

"Boy, you are crazy," Samuel chuckled while shoving fries in his mouth.

"Hey, what is wrong with that?" Frank asked.

"Kids see Santana as some band that their father talks about. Santana wouldn't come back," Samuel laughed.

"Just you wait kid," Frank took a bite of his burger.

"Next you're going to say that the Red Hot Chili Peppers are going to make a comeback," Samuel laughed, biting into another french fry. He saw that Frank was not responding. Samuel turned his head and looked at Frank in disbelief. "Do not tell me you believe that they'll make a comeback too."

"Maybe. I can't predict the future Sam," Frank replied. "Remember, I'm older than you and have gained wisdom."

"Either that or your brain power is starting to fade away," Samuel insulted. "And what happened to 'twenty-nine at heart'?"

2

The two sat in silence for a few moments while eating their dinner. The two had been working together for years. Samuel was only thirty. Despite the age difference, they got along swimmingly. They always managed to get the necessary job done too. Samuel ruffled around in his pocket. After some struggle, a cell phone emerged. He pressed a few buttons as he searched for his voicemails. He saw that he had a voicemail that he had not listened to. So, he held the phone up to his ear to listen.

"Hey Sam, it's me. I just wanted to talk to you about something. Anyways, ah, call me back," said a voicemail on the phone. Loud music was on in the background.

"Did you miss a call from the wife? Prepare for hell when you get home," Frank smiled.

"No, it's my uncle-in-law," Samuel replied. "I could barely understand a word that he said. He has this vinyl record player and he always plays this Metallica record. You'd think that he would turn it off just to speak on the phone right?"

"Well rock and roll doesn't silence for anybody Sam," Frank joked.

"My wife's uncle is staying at our house right now. He's got some financial issues that he needs to work out," Samuel elaborated.

"What kind of financial issues?" Frank asked.

"Well for one thing, he can't live on his own despite the fact that he has a car that is nicer than my house," Samuel complained. He shook his head as he brought another fry to his mouth.

3

"Some people just don't know what to do with their money," Frank reconciled. Frank looked at the phone in Samuel's hand. "Say, is that a new phone?"

"Yeah, it's the Nokia 5110. It's some fancy new cell phone that my wife wanted me to get. She wanted to be able to contact me at all times," Samuel answered.

"Why's that?" Frank asked. "Are you that special?"

"Well if you must know, we are trying to have a baby right now. My wife's logic is that this phone will help with that. It doesn't make any sense to me, but now she needs an excuse to call me at work," Samuel responded. Frank flashed a devilish grin.

"Oh, so someone's been getting busy," Frank chuckled.

"Did you miss the part about her uncle staying with us? Nobody is getting busy in my house Frank," Samuel sighed.

"Well you know what? Kids are nothing but trouble. Anybody in this world who has even one kid is out of their mind, and they need to get their head checked," Frank explained.

"Frank, you have three kids," Samuel replied.

"Exactly," Frank continued. The two continued munching on their burgers and fries. The night was going very smooth and easy. There were no calls all day, which was odd for the town that they lived in. Crime was very prominent in the town, so a day when Samuel and Frank were not called once meant that it was an easy day. It could have been because of the rain, but for whatever reason the town remained quiet. That was, however, until their radio went off.

"All units report to Pigeon Docks immediately. Double homicide reported."

Frank and Samuel gave each other the look that they did when they knew that something was bad. Two people were allegedly killed by the docks. They knew that this was huge. Frank turned the car on, and floored it out of the parking lot with the sirens on. They both tossed their food into the glove compartment.

"Do you know where you're going Frank?" Samuel asked.

"Of course I do. My son goes fishing off of those docks all the time. What's wrong Sam? Are you nervous?" Frank smirked.

"Shit, me? Nervous? You act like you don't even know me. The only thing that scares me is your driving," Samuel answered.

"Well I'm speeding to find out what happened. It's my job," Frank acknowledged. "Also, we are close by and I want to be the first ones there."

"Is that really one of your priorities?" Samuel asked. Frank made a sharp turn, forcing Samuel's head against the window. "Shit, you're going to get us killed. Don't you see how hard it's raining?"

"I want to be the first ones there this time! I've never been the first officer to show up to the scene of a crime before. Don't you want to make a little boy's dream come true?" Frank asked.

The car sped through stop signs. It flew throughout the streets. It then reached the park where the docks were. There were other police sirens blaring in the distance. They were getting closer at a rapid pace. The car parked right in front of the wooden dock where about two dozen boats were stationed. Samuel and Frank stepped out of the car to see what they had been called for.

Off on the wooden dock, there stood a Mexican boy. He appeared to be a young adult. He stood a little shorter than six feet. He was wearing a black rain coat, along with black sweat pants. His shoes were covered in mud. He never glanced at the officers. He just stood there, staring at the two dead bodies at his feet.

"Freeze!" Samuel roared as he raised his pistol at the boy.

"Put your hands in the air!" Frank screamed. The two men were intimidating, but when Samuel tries to be threatening, he is the scariest man on the planet. Three other police vehicles parked near Samuel and Frank's cruiser. The officers in those cars did the same. They jumped out of their cars and raised their pistols at the man standing on the dock. Then, another two cars arrived with more officers who did the same thing. That was when the boy looked away from the bodies, and gave his attention to the police officers aiming at him. He put a gun from his hands into a holster on his hip. He raised his hands in the air to show that he was not armed, nor a threat to them.

"No no no no no no no," he called out to them. Samuel and two other officers rushed forward toward the boy. They were poised to tackle him. "This is a complete misunderstanding! If we can just sit and talk, I can work all of this out!" His words were rushed and filled with fear.

Samuel and the other two officers tackled him to the ground. Samuel got handcuffs around his wrists. The boy did not fight back at all. He just allowed it to happen. He had accepted defeat. One of the officers began reciting the Miranda Rights.

As Samuel led the boy to his police cruiser, he turned his head back towards the two dead bodies. They had both been killed in the same way; a gunshot wound to the back of the head. These men did not see it coming. They were killed in cold blood. The whole situation had filled Samuel's head with so many questions. However, one detail stood out to him about the bodies. One detail stood out like a sore thumb and made Samuel question the whole situation even more.

The dead men were wearing police uniforms.

CHAPTER 2

Samuel walked through the police station. There were various officers crying. The two officers who were shot were Officers Eric Granger and Andrew McFowley. Andrew McFowley had a wife and a child, and another child on the way. Eric Granger was engaged and planning to get married later this year. The two officers had successful careers. They were well liked among the police force. They were respected officers who were taken away too soon. Neither Samuel, nor Frank were very close to the officers, but they had spoken to them before.

Frank walked toward Samuel.

"Any news?" Samuel asked.

"Okay, so the suspect is twenty-two-year old Jonan Casey," Frank answered.

"Have we got him talking yet?" Samuel asked.

"He hasn't said much," Frank answered. "He keeps saying that he ain't no dirty cop killer. Right now, we all think that he is one. Some guys were talking about how much they want to beat him themselves. The cops who are upset aren't allowed to go anywhere near Casey."

"Well is he a dirty cop killer?" Samuel asked.

"He is claiming that he is innocent. I doubt that he is though. This looks real bad for him," Frank continued.

"What did he say when you questioned him?" Samuel asked.

"He refused to answer any of my questions. I questioned him for an hour and he just asked to go to bed. We figured that if we let him get a night of sleep, he could talk to us tomorrow morning," Frank stated. "You know, when he has a clear mind?"

"This is all just a big mess," Samuel sighed.

""I know it is," Frank added.

"These two men had such good lives ahead of them," Samuel continued.

"It's true. This all looks like an easy case. I'm sure that we'll convict him in no time at all," Frank stated. "But I do need your help with something Sam."

"What is it?" Samuel asked.

"Can you be here at nine tomorrow morning to interrogate him?" Frank asked. "You have a way with words and your track record for getting answers is impressive."

"Of course I will. I 'm sure that I can get him talking tomorrow morning," Samuel answered.

"Just be vigilant," Frank began. "The chief is keeping a

tight eye on this guy. He really does not want any officers who were acquainted with the two dead ones to be involved in the case. It makes sense, but it's just weird how close he is staying towards this whole thing."

"It makes sense though," Samuel responded.

"Anyways, go home, get some sleep. You have an important day ahead of you tomorrow Sam," Frank told him. "We're counting on you."

"Thank you. Good night," Samuel turned and left the building. He entered his own car and flipped the key around until the engine roared. The lights inside of the car ignited. The clock read 11:26 pm. His wife was probably asleep by now. Her uncle was a weird guy, so he was probably awake still. The car rolled out of the parking lot and began down the street. The rain had stopped by now and all that remained of it were puddles on the side of the street.

Samuel removed his left hand from the steering wheel and began rubbing his emotionless face. He felt the ridges of the scar on his left cheek. It ran all the way from underneath his eye, down to his lips. He placed his hand back onto the steering wheel. The car's tire splashed through a puddle. The sound of water splashing away from his car and the engine blaring were the only sounds that he could hear. The radio was turned off. Samuel was lost in his thoughts. So many questions ran through his mind. He wanted to know who this kid was. He wanted to know whether or not the kid was guilty. He wanted to know if the kid was dangerous. There were so many questions, but he needed to wait until the next day.

Samuel pulled into the driveway of his suburban home.

He stepped out and locked his car door. He made sure to enter the house silently so as not to wake up his wife. He closed the door behind him. He walked around the living room and into the office. There sat his Uncle in law, Jerry.

"Sammy!" He cheered with gleeful eyes. "It's so good to see you!" Jerry walked over to Samuel and hugged him.

"Good evening Uncle Jerry," Samuel smiled. Jerry backed away from him. Jerry was a fifty-year old black man. He was short and had a face flooded with freckles. He had a small beard that had gone grey. The top of his head was bald, but he had small grey tufts of hair on the sides of his head. He was dwarfed standing next to Samuel. One thing that Samuel always noticed about Jerry was his eyes. The colored part of his eyes were seemingly so large that the white was barely visible.

"Samuel, I have had such a day! I cannot tell you how excited I am for this," Jerry smiled.

"What is it?" Samuel responded. He could barely fake excitement after the day that he had.

"I got a job," Jerry smiled.

"Uncle Jerry that's fantastic," Samuel smiled. *So now you can get out of my house?*

"Yup. I have a job now. I am going to be selling these revolutionary vacuums that will change the way that people clean," Jerry smiled. His excitement was palpable. "My friend invented this kind of vacuum that has a hose and a compartment on it for water and cleaning solution. So you spray the spill with the cleaning solution, then suck that up, then spray it with water, then suck that up too. I'm going to be selling those!"

"Well then I am going to be your first customer," Samuel laughed.

"Thank you," Jerry smiled. "We have to celebrate." Jerry rushed to his suitcase and removed a box. The box contained ten compartments for cigars, but there were two slots that were empty. Jerry removed two more cigars from the container and handed one to Samuel.

"Well, I'm sure that my wife wouldn't have a problem with me smoking," Samuel commented. "Thank you Jerry."

"No Sammy, thank you," Jerry clipped off the ends of the cigars and lit them. Jerry took a deep inhale on his. He then blew out a puff of smoke. "Thank you for letting me live in your house for the past few months."

"Oh don't sweat it. You're family Jerry. You can stay here however long you want," Samuel answered.

"Well, I'm going to be moving out to live on my own now," Jerry announced. Samuel looked shocked.

"Jerry that is amazing. I'm so happy for you," Samuel marveled.

"Get this, the store that I'm going to be working at is in Arizona. So I'm going to be moving across the whole country," Jerry revealed. This took Samuel back.

"Oh my God. So how often will we get to see you?" Samuel asked.

"I'll definitely visit you guys every now and then," Jerry answered. "I'm going to be making a lot of money now from this. My friend promised me that."

"Hopefully enough to take care of that car of yours," Samuel blew out a puff of smoke. Jerry began laughing.

"Yeah I couldn't help myself when I saw that beautiful thing. I knew that it was out of my price range, but I just couldn't help myself," Jerry laughed. He took a puff on his cigar. Then, he exhaled through his nose. "Now that I'm working again, I need to get myself a new coat."

"What happened to the brown overcoat?" Samuel asked. "You just wore it yesterday."

"Oh that thing is ruined now. Some idiot on the bus spilled food on it and it stained," Jerry answered. Samuel studied the cigar in his hand.

"Say, what kind of cigars are these?" Samuel asked.

"They are Colombian. You see, so many people are too focused on the buzz around Cuban cigars, that they gloss over Colombian beauties," Jerry answered. "Sometimes, we focus too much on what we are looking for, that we forget about where we should look."

"I've never had a Colombian cigar before," Samuel said, inhaling on the cigar.

"Well, they are far better than Cubans, I can tell you that," Jerry continued. "So how was your day Sammy?"

"Oh don't get me started. I can't tell you too much, but I think that this kid got himself into big trouble," Samuel sighed. Jerry's posture and facial expression changed into one of concern and perplexity.

"Oh really? Tell me more," Jerry pressed.

"Well, I can't tell you much. It just looks really bad for this kid right now. We are all pretty much certain that he committed a horrible crime," Samuel elaborated.

"Well, don't go into this with your mind made up already," Jerry advised. "If one looks for evil in places that it does not exist, he will trick himself into believing that he has found it."

"Yeah that's cute Uncle Jerry, but I don't know if that will help me," Samuel responded. Jerry stood up and walked towards the vinyl player in the back of the office next to a window. He ran his fingers along the metallic surface. "Say, what did you call me about?"

"Oh that?" Jerry asked. "That was about the job that I got. I wanted to let you know. Monica does not know that I'm moving yet, so don't tell her. It's a surprise." Jerry stepped towards the desk in the office. Samuel always noticed how Jerry would walk throughout the room in a certain pattern. He would start at the back corner where the vinyl player and the window were, then move to the desk, then he would step outside of the room right next to the entrance, then he would finish by walking back to the corner where the vinyl player was.

"I could barely hear a damn word that you said when the music was blaring," Samuel chuckled. Jerry stepped outside of the room and positioned himself next to the entrance of the room, just as Samuel predicted.

"What can I say?" Jerry responded, as he began stepping back towards the vinyl player. "'Master of Puppets' is my favorite song."

"Well maybe it can be turned off for a second while you're on the phone?" Samuel joked. Jerry smiled.

"Uh, no," Jerry laughed. He took a breath of the cigar in his hand.

"I should go to bed now Jerry. I have an important day ahead of me tomorrow. Thanks for the cigar," Samuel handed it back to Jerry. "Congrats on the new job. When do you leave?"

"Tomorrow night," Jerry smiled.

"I am so happy for you. I really am," Samuel smiled. "Good night."

"Good night."

Samuel walked up the stairs quietly. He stepped into his bedroom, where his wife Monica lay in bed fast asleep. Quietly, in order to not awake her, Samuel changed into his pajamas. He then delicately laid down. He shut his eyes in anticipation of the day that was ahead of him.

CHAPTER 3

"Why are you so dressed up?" Monica asked, eyeing Samuel's suit and tie. "What's the occasion?"

"Well, if you must know, I am questioning somebody today. I thought that this would be fitting," Samuel responded. He stared at himself in the mirror in their room. He admired the way that he looked in a suit. "I look pretty damn good in a suit. I should wear these more." Samuel acknowledged.

"I wouldn't mind that one bit," She grinned. "What are you questioning somebody about?"

"Some idiot allegedly shot two cops," Samuel responded. "I say 'allegedly' but it is pretty obvious that he did it."

"Oh my God! Did you know either of them?" Monica asked, gripping her brown hair.

"Not really. That's why I am the man questioning this kid. It's because I'll be less bias than somebody who knew the cops," Samuel answered. Monica placed one hand on her chest nervously.

"How is Frank holding up? Did he know them?" She asked.

"Oh don't worry about Frank. He's a big boy. He can take care of himself. He didn't know them either," Samuel explained. "Now don't you get too stressed out. I don't think that getting nervous and anxious will help us have a baby."

"You're right. You're right," Monica agreed.

"Don't even think about it," Samuel advised.

"Don't even think about what?" Monica asked smiling.

"Exactly," Samuel smiled. He stepped out of the room to walk downstairs, but he bumped into Jerry who was stepping out of the upstairs bathroom. "What in the hell? Uncle Jerry you scared the hell outta me. You were so quiet I didn't even hear you."

"Oh, I'm sorry Samuel. I'll make more noise next time. I had to use the john," Jerry smiled. Samuel got nervous for a moment. It was bad enough that he told his wife about the officer's getting shot, but he did not want Jerry to know either. He knew that the police chief liked to keep things like this private for some bit of time until he knew that it was safe to tell news outlets. Something like this getting leaked too soon in the investigation would not be good.

"Uncle Jerry, you didn't hear anything that we said in there to each other, did you?" Samuel asked. Jerry made a face at Samuel.

"Oh Sammy, you can't hide anything from me," Jerry said sternly. Samuel felt like he was going to start sweating beads. Jerry placed one hand on Samuel's shoulder. His face cracked a smile. "Oh Sam, why didn't you tell me that you two were trying to have a baby?"

"I'm so sorry Uncle Jerry. We just wanted to keep this private for a while," It was difficult to contain his sigh of relief. But then one question poked at Samuel; who would he rather have mad at him, his boss, or his wife?

"Oh, don't worry about it kiddo. I am so proud of you two," Jerry continued. Monica walked out the door.

"What are you proud of?" Monica asked, feeling concerned.

"You two are having a baby!" Jerry exclaimed. Monica gave Samuel a dirty look.

"I wonder how Uncle Jerry knew that," Monica placed both of her hands on her hips while eyeing Samuel.

"Well I have an announcement too," Jerry revealed. "I'm moving tonight!"

"Tonight?" Monica screeched.

"Sam didn't tell you?" Jerry asked.

"No, he didn't," Monica crossed her arms and eyed Samuel. Samuel looked at his wrist.

"Oh my goodness look at the time. I need to go now or else I'm going to be late," Samuel said.

"Sam, you aren't wearing a watch," Monica scolded.

"Good bye. I love you," Samuel kissed Monica. He then turned and shook Jerry's hand. After that, he was out the door. Samuel got into his car and drove off. He was on his way to a day filled with hours of questioning. He was ready for it. He had been training for this for years. He had never fronted an interrogation like this. He was looking forward to it, and dreading it all at the same time. He needed to face the person who took the lives of two police officers.

He pulled into the parking lot of the police station. He exited the car and felt the cool March air. There were puddles all around from the rain the previous night. He walked from the parking lot into the police station.

"Sam, big day ahead of you?" Frank greeted. He extended a cup of coffee to Samuel.

"No thanks Frank," Samuel responded with one hand up.

"Whatever, more for me then," Frank responded, sipping the cup.

"What room am I supposed to talk to this kid in?" Samuel asked.

"Cutting right to the chase I see," Frank said. "Follow me."

Frank led Samuel down a series of hallways. They walked throughout the building for a minute. That was until they got to the end of a hallway. The walls were untouched concrete, which was only decorated with iron clad doors. Frank pointed at one of the doors.

"Check to see what wonders lay behind door number two," Frank smiled. Samuel did not smile back. "I get it. You're in a bad mood."

"Before I go in, what is it that we know about this guy?"

Samuel asked.

"Everything that I already told you. We don't have anything new," Frank answered. "His name is Jonan Casey. Have fun with that."

"Oh it is going to be a long day," Samuel sighed.

"There are cameras in the room so you don't need to worry about writing everything down. Just ask him questions and get the answers that we need," Frank assured. "If you can get a confession out of him, then we are all done. Sending him to jail would be open and shut."

"Wish me luck," Samuel requested. He turned and stepped inside. He closed the door behind him. He was now in the den of the beast. In the room was a table, and two chairs. One of the chairs was empty. That chair was for Samuel. The other chair held the suspect, Jonan Casey. He was handcuffed to the table so he would not be able to move around too much. He was Mexican. He was scrawny and had no facial hair. His hair was dark and short. His eyes were glassy and brown. His nose jutted out of his face. It was a huge nose. It was oddly shaped too. It resembled the tail of an airplane. Jonan looked up at Samuel.

"My name is officer Samuel Delcastillo. You are twenty-two-year old Jonan Casey," Samuel greeted.

"The pleasure is all mine," Jonan gave a cocky smile. "You were one of the officers that tackled me. I recognize you. You have one hell of a tackle dude. Were you on the football team in high school?"

"I'm not your 'dude', son," Samuel snapped. "And yes I played football."

"Alright, I know that you probably have a ton of questions for me. But I am here to tell you that all of those questions are irrelevant," Jonan assured.

"You are dreaming boy," Samuel chuckled.

"Alright then. One of your questions was going to be something along the lines of 'did you kill those cops?' Well I can tell you with confidence that I am not any dirty old cop killer. I have never killed anyone in my life," Jonan stated.

"Right now, I don't quite know about that boy," Samuel responded.

"Wait wait wait. You didn't let me finish," Jonan put one finger up. "I have done illegal things and I will admit to all of those terrible things that I have done. But the thing is, I have never in my life killed anyone. That is true. That is a fact."

"Well it shouldn't come as a surprise to you that I find that a little difficult to believe right now," Samuel responded.

"That only makes sense. I understand what you mean. It looks very bad for me right now," Jonan continued.

"Wow, you must have an IQ of two hundred. Did you figure that out on your own?" Samuel asked.

"I appreciate the sarcasm tough guy," Jonan said. "I have thought about this long and hard overnight. I have decided that it is in my best interest to tell you the whole story."

"Well, we have all day to talk," Samuel responded.

"Now here is the thing. Much of this story will seem completely irrelevant. I just need you to stick with it. It is a long and convoluted story that lead me to Thursday night, standing above two dead police officers. I just need for you to listen to me. I need you to listen to the whole story. I promise that every detail that I will give you is relevant. Can you do that for me?" Jonan asked.

"I am all ears," Samuel responded. Jonan smiled.

"Here we go."

So my story begins on New Year's Day. 1997 was over and in comes 1998. This was back when I had a flowing beard that made me look like a God. You see, at the time I was dating this girl. Her name was Chelsea. She was a wonderful person and our relationship had been going on for a good solid year. We were living together. I worked for her father at his architecture company. I was an accountant for him. It was a nice gig and paid well. Her family was awesome. Her dad liked me, her mom liked me, and her sister Melanie liked me. You don't understand, I really mean that Melanie liked me. She liked me a lot.

That's probably the reason that Melanie and I had drunken sex on New Year's Eve night. Damn was that strange. She looked just like Chelsea, but had a deeper voice. The next morning I woke up with a hangover, Melanie in the bed next to me, and Chelsea downstairs. I walked downstairs with the hope that Chelsea did not know.

"Good morning," I greeted. She did not seem angry, so I thought that I was in the clear.

"You fucked my sister you jackass!" After she yelled that, I began to suspect that she knew.

"You seem mad," I began.

"Oh do I?" She screamed.

"I get the feeling that you are upset with me," I continued.

"You fucked my sister!" She insisted.

"I didn't mean to. It was an accident," I answered.

"How do you accidentally fuck my sister?" She belted.

"Chelsea, baby, you are mad but there is a perfectly logical explanation for this. I was drunk," I felt relieved after I said that. It felt like that was the keystone to any argument. Flash the "I was drunk" excuse and any issue would be solved.

"That doesn't solve this issue at all!"

Dammit, I was wrong again. I'm not good at reading people, I guess.

"Relax. I have only had sex with your sister like twice," I added. Her eyes went wide.

"This wasn't the first time?" She sounded angry.

"Well, last year on your birthday we were all drinking-" my sentence was cut short due to the fact that an empty beer bottle collided with my jaw. I stepped back grabbing my face. "I think that that was a little out of line."

"I have never been madder at you before Jonan!" She continued. My mind raced. I looked for anything that could help me in a situation like this. She was mad, but there had to be some kind of outside source that was making her more upset than she really was. There had to be something else that was irritating her that was out of my control. Then I realized that it was the beginning of the month. I know what that usually means.

"Now Chelsea, do you think that you aren't really mad at me? Do you think that maybe you are irritable because you are on your period right now?" I suggested.

"Boy you are a special kinda stupid aren't you?" Samuel interrupted.

"You're interrupting my story," Jonan replied.

"I have been married for five years and nobody had to tell me to never ever under any circumstances suggest that she is only mad because of the fact that she was on her period. I never had to learn it the hard way, I just knew that that was a huge mistake," Samuel continued.

"That was probably why she threw the second bottle at me."

The second bottle collided with the wall behind me. I ducked so that it wouldn't hit me. I was ready for this one. I knew that she was throwing things at that moment so I was prepared.

"Chelsea, I kinda have a headache from the hangover, so if you could just turn down the screaming, and the shattering of bottles, that'd be great," I suggested.

"If you could get out of my life that'd be great!" Chelsea responded.

"Should I go?" I asked.

"Never come back here. I never want to see you again!" Chelsea yelled. So I walked out the front door in my robe and slippers. But halfway down the driveway, I had a thought. Before I left Chelsea for the last time, I needed to ask her something. There was something that I just couldn't leave in that apartment. Something needed to be taken care of. So I walked back into the apartment proudly with my head held high. I looked at Chelsea and I got it off of my chest.

"Chelsea, before I leave," I began. "I left a six pack in the fridge. Mind if I take it with me?"

I'll spare you the details on the rest of that conversation. The main point is that it was a lot more yelling. So I grabbed my suit, and I left. After all, I still had to go to work that day. I knew that it was going to be awkward since I worked for Chelsea's father. I was nervous. My knees were shaking. Chelsea had the car, so I had to walk to work. As soon as I did, Chelsea's father called me into his office. I knew that that conversation would not end well. I sat down in a chair that was across the desk from him. My boss looked upset.

"Jonan, do you know why I called you down here?" He asked.

"Is it because you enjoy my company?" I asked.

"No. I can promise you that that is the opposite of why you are here," He continued. "I can't believe this. I invite you into my home, I treat you with nothing but hospitality, I give you a job, and what do you do? You fuck my daughters, and you are a failure in every way, shape and form. What do you have to say for yourself?"

"I would like to ask for a raise," I responded. He leaned forward.

"You're fired," He answered. I can't say that I entirely did not see it coming.

"So do you want me to come in again sometime for my last paycheck?" I asked.

"You know what? I never want to see your sorry ass again," He began. "So I took the liberty of taking all of the money that I owe you, and put it in an envelope in cash. That way, I never have to see you again. Sound good?"

"That seems reasonable," I responded. He handed me an envelope.

"Here. This contains every cent that I owe you. Five hundred seventeen dollars and seventeen cents," He stated. "Now we are square. You know what that means right?"
"What?" I asked.

"Get, the fuck, out of my life," He instructed.

"What do I do for money?" I asked.

"I don't care. Leave," He responded.

"Do you think that maybe you are being a little bit unreasonable?" I asked. That was about the point when he called security guards to throw me out.

So there I was. I was homeless, unemployed, without a car, and only had five hundred seventeen dollars and seventeen cents to my name. The world was my oyster.
••

"You know what boy, I said this once and I'll say it again; you are a special kind of stupid," Samuel interrupted.

"Officer, you are making it difficult for me to tell you my

story. Are you trying to insult me? Because I feel insulted right now," Jonan replied. "Do you want me to tell my story or not?"

"Why the hell did you ask that man for a raise?" Samuel asked.

"I figured that he was going to punish me. What better way to punish me than to deny my request for a raise? I thought that then maybe I wouldn't get fired," Jonan continued.

"How did that work out for you?" Samuel smiled.

"Real funny hot shot," Jonan smirked. "Do you want me to finish my story now?"

"Yes keep going. I'll stay quiet," Samuel answered.

"Thank you," Jonan sat back. "Where was I again?"

"The world was your oyster," Samuel answered.

"Ah yes, the world was my oyster."

So the world was my oyster. I wandered the streets for hours until I was in the next town. Everyone in the town I had lived in before knew me as the sexy man who was dating Chelsea. But now, I was just the sexy man. I needed to find a place where I wasn't known. I needed to find somewhere that nobody knew me. I was going to start my new life over in this New Year. I was going to start my new life with only five hundred seventeen dollars and seventeen cents. So, needless to say, it was going to be an uphill battle. With the sadness of a breakup, and my recent unemployment, that night I went to a bar. It was the most pretentious bar that I have ever seen. It was so out of place too. It was in this really shady part of town, but looked like it belonged in Beverly Hills. It was called "The Monocle" which only added to its pretentiousness. But all I wanted to do was get drunk so I accepted it.

I stepped into the bar and looked around at the drink selections. It was a Friday night, so the bar was absolutely packed. One of the drinks was called a "feeling drowner", so I decided to give into the pretentiousness and order one.

"That will be seventeen dollars seventeen cents," The bartender said.

"I only ordered one of them," I replied.

"That is the price of one of them," He added.

"Oh, well then I don't want one. Sorry," After I said that, the bartender turned away. I was really good at disappointing people that day. I turned to leave, but then somebody put one hand on my shoulder. I turned to see that out of the ocean of drunk people around me, this scrawny white guy was trying to get my attention.

"Hey buddy, are you looking for a good time?" He asked.

"I guess so," I responded. I really was looking for a good time. I was hoping to drown my sadness in alcohol, but I was going to give this guy a shot. He held up a small plastic baggy filled with a white powder.

"Five hundred dollars for the best night of your life," The man continued. Five hundred dollars for the best night of my life sounded too good to be true. So I decided to decline.

"I'm sorry but-" midsentence, the mathematician inside of me went off. The drink at the bar was seventeen dollars and seventeen cents. The cocaine that this man was offering me was five hundred dollars. I had exactly five hundred, seventeen dollars, and seventeen cents in my pocket. This was the cosmos telling me what to do. No, this was something more than that. This was destiny. The mathematical probability of this happening by chance was slim to none. No, this had to have been divine intervention. God made himself known to me on that night. The planets had aligned to show me to this moment. God was telling me to spend the last pennies that I had on a Feeling Drowner and a baggy of cocaine. "On second thought, I'll take it." I smiled.

"Awesome," The man smiled. I gave the man five hundred dollars. Then I turned to the bartender and ordered that fancy expensive drink. I looked back at the man who sold me the cocaine.

"What's your name?" I asked.

"Ned. You?" He responded.

"Jonan," I answered.

"Well Jonan, now that you have your own cocaine, I invite you to do lines with me," Ned offered. I smiled.

"Of course I'll do lines with you."

And so I took my fancy drink, and went to do lines of cocaine with Ned. Little did I know that that moment would alter every moment for the rest of my year.

CHAPTER 4

"So let me get this straight," Samuel began. "You have just admitted to me that you have done cocaine?"

"Come on Officer, I told you before I started that I would admit to every crime that I've committed," Jonan answered. "And I'm not done admitting to other crimes that I've done."

"So you spent every last dime that you had on booze and cocaine?" Samuel asked.

"What you call 'booze and cocaine' Ned called 'the best night of my life'. In hindsight, I probably should not have bought cocaine and booze because it kick started the domino effect that lead me to where we are now. Also, impulse buying the day of a breakup usually leads to regret," Jonan continued.

"Do you not have any common sense boy? Didn't you go to high school?" Samuel asked. Jonan chuckled.

"Oh give me a break Officer. They don't teach you common sense in high school," Jonan scoffed.

"So what did you do after you realized that you had no money?" Samuel asked.

"One thing lead to another and I shot two cops in the head," Jonan replied. Samuel glared at him. "It's called sarcasm officer. You should learn it. I intended to lighten the mood. You don't come off as the fun type to me."

"Is this a joke to you or something?" Samuel demanded.

"Wow you are tense. You should laugh more," Jonan advised.

"Can you continue on with your story?" Samuel asked.

"I've done enough storytelling. How did you get that scar on your face?" Jonan asked.

"The story Casey. Continue the goddamn story," Samuel stammered.

"Alright fine," Jonan answered. "So the memories of the rest of that night are foggy. I do remember that it was the happiest that I had ever been though. I don't remember what went on, but I do remember waking up the next morning."

•••

I woke up in a hotel room. I was on the floor of the hotel room for some reason. There were two beds, a bathroom, a nightstand next to each bed, and a television that was playing a Lynard Skynard concert. I believe that the song playing was "That Smell". I stood up and wiped the drool from my face. I was wearing all of my clothes from the night before. They were drenched in sweat and drool. The room was brightly lit with the lamps on. The walls were bright yellow with twisted lines of green all over the walls. I looked to the beds. One of them was neatly made, while the other one had the sheets all torn up despite the fact that no one was in it. Then, the bathroom door opened and there was Ned.

"Glad to see that you're awake."

"Um, Ned?" I asked.

"What is it champ?" Ned responded.

"Do you remember anything that happened last night?" I asked, scratching the crust out of my eyes.

"Oh I remember everything crystal clear," Ned laughed.

"What did we do?" I asked. My mouth was bone dry.

"We had some fucking party!" Ned chuckled. He walked back into the bathroom. He left the door open as he began brushing his teeth. "So wha har bar huhar?"

"What?" I asked. He spit out his toothpaste.

"So what are your plans now?" Ned asked. I scratched my head. I had no idea what my plans were. I had no money. I had no place to go. I had no job. I had nothing but the clothes on my back, and Ned's toothy grin in front of me.

"I don't know. I don't have any plans," I answered.

"Where are you going to go?" Ned asked. He put the tooth brush back in his mouth and started brushing again.

"I don't know. I don't have a job, or a home right now," I explained. Ned spit the toothpaste in his mouth into the sink.

"Do you need a job?" Ned asked. I shrugged.

"I guess so," I replied. Ned went into the drawer of the

bathroom vanity and pulled out a pen. He also pulled out a roll of toilet paper. He wrote something on it and handed it to me. There was a phone number on the toilet paper.

"Here. Later today, call this number and tell them that Ned sent you." Obviously, there was nothing suspicious about this. What could possibly go wrong? Getting handed a phone number by a man that I had just met, and did lines of cocaine with the night before seemed like a perfectly reasonable place to seek employment.

"Will do. Thanks Ned," I replied. I took the phone number in my hand. I looked back at him. "How do I call this number? I don't have a phone, or money to use a payphone."

"I got you," Ned replied. He walked toward the corner of the room where his coat was. He reached into the pocket and removed four quarters. He walked back to me and placed them in my hand. "Here is money for a payphone. Use it wisely Jonan."

"Thank you," I answered.

"I'm sure that we have a long friendship ahead of us," Ned smiled. I opened the door to leave. I looked at him before I left.

"That sounds nice. I could really use a friend right now," I smiled. I turned and left.

Thank God I never saw that lunatic again. That guy was freaking weird. Good riddance Ned. I wouldn't want to spend another minute of my life with that guy even if the lives of a dozen orphans depended on it. Gross.

I took the elevator downstairs. I walked up to the front

desk in an attempt to figure out where the hell I was. I walked over to the attendant lady.

"Excuse me miss, what is the address of this hotel?" I asked. The woman smiled at me.

"Eighty-Three Freehold Way," The woman smiled. That was good. I knew where I was. Also, I was still in my home town.

"Thank you," I replied.

"Did you enjoy your stay?" She asked. She was smiling a lot and making a weird amount of eye contact with me. It was gross. I dislike people like that. If I don't know someone, why do they act like we are friends?

"Um... yeah," I responded.

"Well I certainly enjoyed your stay Jonan," She winked at me. That was when it clicked in my head. She seemed genuinely attracted to me and interested in me.

"Have a nice day." I took the opportunity to leave. I left the hotel and began my journey. I had a phone number in my pocket and the intention to call that phone number. But first, I needed to find a payphone. I'll spare you the details, but it took me way longer to find a payphone than I had hoped. It wasn't like I was in any sort of a rush to be somewhere though. I didn't have anywhere to be.

Eventually I found one. I placed two quarters in the slot, and then dialed the phone number scribbled on the toilet paper. I took the phone in my hand and held it to my face. The ringing was clear as day. It only rang for a moment before it was answered.

"Who gave you this number?" A woman on the other end answered. I stumbled with my words.

"Ned did," I responded.

"What did you call here for?" The woman asked.

"I seek employment," I responded.

"Tomorrow afternoon go to the Stuarts' Tavern. Be there at three fifteen. Sit on the bar stool fourth to the left. At exactly three thirty, order a shot of whiskey. I will make myself known to you and then we talk. Understand?" She asked.

"Yes understood. I know where that bar is," I answered.

"Any questions?" She asked.

"Yeah. Will you pay for my shot of whiskey?" I asked.

"Of course. Any other questions?" She asked.

"Nope," I replied.

"Good. See you then," She then hung up. So I hung up the phone too.

And there it was. I knew what the plan was. The bar that she had mentioned was not too far from where I was. Our scheduled meeting was not for another twenty-four hours. So for the rest of the day I hung out at a children's park. Nobody was there all day except for me. I was starving by that night. I had two quarters in my pocket. I couldn't get any food with that, nor was I motivated enough to find food. I tried to fall asleep on the slide, but the night was cold. I was shivering all night. I still don't understand how I managed to fall asleep. It was a miracle.

That night I dreamed. I dreamt of Chelsea. For some reason, I dreamt of that Christmas. I dreamt of spending it with her family. She always told me about how much she wanted to take a boy to the family Christmas party to show off. Her siblings and cousins always had their dates. She was beaming a huge grin when we got there. I've never seen her happier than when I shook hands with her grandpa. It was a nice dream. Seeing Chelsea smile made me happy.

Until I was awakened that morning by some brat poking me with a stick.

"Excuse me sir, why are you sleeping on the slide?" He asked. His mom ran over to him. She grabbed his arm and pulled him away from me.

"Timmy, don't talk to him," She advised.

"Mommy, does God love the homeless?" He asked her.

"No he doesn't sweetie," She replied, carrying him away from the park.

I realized just how much I smelled. I reeked of smells that I did not even recognize. I had a headache, and my back was killing me. But now that I was awake, I needed to go to the place of hopes and dreams; Stuarts Tavern.

I managed to make it there on time. When I walked into the bar, the clock read three eleven. The stool by the bar that was fourth to the left was open, so I sat down. I eyed every person in the bar. I couldn't tell which woman was the one that I spoke to on the phone. When the clock was at three sixteen, the bartender walked over to me.

"Can I help you?" He asked.

"I'm still deciding," I responded. It wasn't three thirty yet, so I couldn't order the whiskey yet. The bartender asked me every few minutes if I was ready to order, and I am sure that it bugged him every time I replied with "I don't know yet.".

Finally, three thirty rolled around and I ordered my drink. It was so strange. Immediately after the bartender put it down, the seat to my left was occupied by a woman in a blue dress. Oh my God, I had never seen a better looking woman in my life. She was sexy by every definition of the word. Her long straight hair went all the way down to her hips. It was black as midnight. Her complexion was perfect. Not a wrinkle or a blemish on her face. Her eyes were a dark blue. She was white, but not so white that she looked like a ghost. She had the perfect hourglass figure too. The blue dress left her arms and shoulders bare. Her breasts were bigger than any I had ever seen in my life on a girl her size. I mean they were-
■■

"I get it," Samuel interrupted.

"But you don't understand," Jonan answered.

"Thank you Jonan. I get it," Samuel replied.

"You would want to see them," Jonan stated.

"No I don't," Samuel replied.

"Well you're missing out man," Jonan said.

"Please continue with your story," Samuel insisted. "And don't call me 'man'."
■■

"My name is Arabella," She introduced herself. She extended her hand to shake mine. I shook her hand.

"We spoke over the phone," I began.

"Correct," Arabella replied. Even her name was sexy. "Do you seek employment?"

"Yes," I answered. She held a piece of paper, a clipboard, and a pen.

"What is your first and last name?" She asked.

"Jonan Casey," I answered. She wrote down on the paper. She held it so that I could not see what she was writing.

"Current occupation?"

"Unemployed."

"Marital status?"

"Single."

"Phone number?"

"I don't have a phone."

"Address?"

"Homeless," I answered. "Is that an issue?"

"Not at all. That is even better," Arabella replied. She removed a piece of paper from her purse and handed it to me. "I need you to get to a pay phone. At eight thirty tonight, you need to call the number on this paper. You will speak to my employer directly. Then he will give you a job."

"Wait, so I got a job?" I was shocked. She asked me a few personal questions and instantly I have a job. It was super sketchy, but hey, I had a job. She pulled out two twenty dollar bills and handed them to me.

"Pay for your drink, find a place to stay tonight, and take a damn shower for Christ's sake." Arabella instructed.

"Uh, sure," I answered. And so she left. That was not the last that I would see of Arabella.

So I paid for my drink and left. I found a cheap motel to stay at overnight. I showered, and washed my clothes in the shower with me so that I wouldn't have to pay for a washing machine rental. I hung them up to dry. Then, I sat in that dirty cheap motel room for a few hours doing basically nothing. It was nice to be in a warm room rather than the cold outside. The motel room had a landline, so when eight thirty came around, I dialed the number that Arabella gave me. The phone barely rang for a second until it was answered.

"Who gave you this number?" The man on the other end had a very deep and threatening voice. He sounded older than me, but I couldn't tell.

"Arabella," I replied.

"You spoke with her today?" He asked.

"Yes. I was seeking employment," I stated.

"Tomorrow, go outside Stuart's Tavern at exactly eleven in the morning. Do not be late. A car will come to pick you up. A girl will ask you what your name is. You will tell her that your name is Mason. You are not to tell her your real name under any circumstances. Do you understand me?" The man asked.

"Do not tell her my real name under any circumstances. Got it," I replied.

"You are not to tell her any personal information about yourself such as where you live, or your phone number. You are not to ask for this person's real name. They will tell you a pseudonym. Call her by the name that she tells you to. You are not to attempt to get personal information from her. Your relationship with her will be strictly professional. Do everything exactly as she instructs. Do you understand?" He asked.

"Yes," I replied.

"Good," He then hung up.

The joke was on him. I don't have an address or phone number to tell this woman.

CHAPTER 5

So there I was, Stuart's Tavern street corner at ten fifty-nine in the morning. All that I had eaten in a day was a hot dog that I bought from some food cart for a dollar. After the motel room, the hot dog, and the drink, I had two dollars and thirty-seven cents left. I counted that amount over and over again until it was burned into my brain permanently. I still remember it. That was enough money to buy another hot dog with thirty-eight cents to spare. So with all of the money that I had left I could afford a hot dog and a gumball. So my situation was shitty to say the least.

Despite my poverty, I had work that day. I did not know what to expect. All that I knew was that I was going to do a job that probably involved cocaine. It was my only option. The only clothes that I had left were the clothes on my back; a suit with dress pants, a pair of socks, and a pair of shoes. I was freezing, and my suit was a wrinkled mess. No one in their right mind would hire me. This was my only option. If I didn't get paid, then I wouldn't be able to eat. Also, I think that I would rather get hit by a car than have to sleep on another slide again.

That was when a car pulled up right in front of me. It was a black sedan. It looked like a car that my grandfather would drive. It certainly didn't look like the type of car a criminal would be driving. The window rolled down. A girl was sitting in the driver's seat. She was a white girl, her hair was brown, her eyes were green, her teeth were white as marshmallows, her cheeks had a lot of freckles on them. She was wearing a green sweater and jeans. She did not look like a person I would expect to be involved in the drug business. Also, after seeing her teeth I started to think about marshmallows, and suddenly I was hungry again.

"What's your name?" She asked. The man that I had spoken to on the phone the night before told me to use the name "Kevin" when I spoke with her. I remembered that. The guy on the phone did not want this girl to know anything about me, and I assumed that she would give me a false name as well.

"Kevin," I said with a wink.

"Get in Kevin," She said sternly. So I hopped in. After I closed the door behind me, she began to drive off.

"So what's the plan?" I asked. She turned the street corner.

"Well, I need to ask you a few questions first," she said.

"Shoot."

"Who have you spoken to thus far?" She asked me. I thought back to the day before.

"I spoke to some weirdo Ned, I spoke to this breathtaking woman Arabella, and some dude with a deep voice over the phone," I responded. The girl smirked.

"Yeah, Ned is pretty freaking weird," She agreed. "The man that you spoke to over the phone is our employer."

"Alright. He seemed like a chill guy," I stated.

"He is not, and you better not tell him that," She snapped. I decided that it wouldn't be a good idea to ask questions about him anymore. "Why do you want to work with us?"

"Uh, well, I guess that I need the money," I answered.

"Why do you need the money?" She asked.

"Well, as of right now I am homeless. I own two dollars and thirty-seven cents right now. To be honest, I'm desperate," I responded.

"Good to know. Do you have any kids?" She asked. I laughed out loud.

"Kids? Are you nuts? Anyone who wants to have a child is insane. Those things are just disease buckets, and I don't have health insurance. Also, if I just told you that I have two dollars and thirty-seven cents to my name, why on earth would you think that I have a kid?" I laughed. That made her smile for about a half second. I considered it a victory.

"Do you have any close family members?" She asked.

"Not anymore. I'm kind of a loner," I replied. "I don't even have any friends."

"So how did you get into this homeless situation?" She asked.

"Well, I lost my girlfriend, and my job, and my home all in the same day. So for the last two nights I've slept on a slide, and in a cheap ass motel room. The average person would call me homeless. I am an optimist, so I like to call myself a rolling stone," I explained.

"And a pessimist would call you a bum," She stated.

"I was dancing around that word but thanks for saying it," I smirked.

"Have you ever done anything illegal?" She asked.

"Nope. I am an asshole, but I've never broken the law," I lied. I may have also done cocaine, but I left that detail out.

"Do you know anyone in any gangs?" She asked. That was when my heart jumped. I sat up.

"Wait, I'm not going to be getting into gang fights am I? I'm not dying like that kid from 'The Outsiders'. I-"

"We aren't getting into any gang fights. I was just asking if you knew anyone in a gang," She continued.

"You women ask too many damn questions," I responded. "And no, I do not know anyone in any gangs. Can it be my turn to ask a question now? I don't even know your name."

"Natalie," She lied. I knew that that wasn't her real name. It was definitely a pseudonym. "Do you know any police officers?"

"Natalie, I just told you that I don't have any friends or close family members. Zero out of the zero people that I know are cops," I answered.

"You've got a mouth on you," Natalie replied. "I like that."

"Thank you. I like me too," I joked. Natalie was still driving and I had no idea where we were going. "So now can you tell me what the plan is?"

"Well, you and I are going to be selling," She began.

"Selling?"

"Yes, selling."

"That tells me nothing. What are we selling?" I asked.

"Drugs." She answered.

"Gee, I thought that we were selling lollipops," I mocked. "What kind of drugs?"

"Why? Do you plan on using them?" She turned it around on me.

"Fuck that. I never want to touch any dope again for as long as I live," I answered.

"Well then good. It is important that there is no temptation. Our employer doesn't like people who steal from him," she continued. "Also, I'm going to need you to shave that beard of yours."

"What?" I asked.

"The beard. It needs to go," Natalie responded. I put one hand over my beard.

"Um, no," I answered.

"Um, yes," Natalie snapped.

"The beard is part of my essence. It's part of my soul. The beard is part of me. I am part of the beard. He has been my testosterone friend through good times and bad. If you make me shave the beard, then you strip me of who I am," I bargained.

"Kevin, our employer does not like beards," Natalie explained.

"Well that is too bad for him," I argued.

"Well, if that beard is part of your essence, is a baggy suit and the smell of a dead water buffalo also part of your essence?" Natalie asked.

"Well now you've turned this into a personal thing," I slumped into my seat. I sat there scratching my beard for a few minutes. We sat in the car until I broke the silence again a few minutes later. "So what is the plan?"

"Well Kevin, we are going to be selling drugs. We have to drive to a location where another car awaits us. There, we will switch cars. That car has the product in the trunk. Then, we drive that car to the meeting point where we will meet some men. We'll sell the product to them, and then we drive back to the original car. We'll get back into this one, and then I'll drive you back to Stuart's tavern," Natalie explained.

"Why do we switch cars?" I asked.

"For the sake of anonymity. The less the men that we are selling to know about us the better," Natalie explained.

"So why go through all of this trouble to sell a petty amount of drugs?" I asked.

"We aren't selling a petty amount. Our employer wants us to sell in bulk," Natalie explained.

"Define 'in bulk'," I requested.

"Three kilograms," Natalie replied. I laughed.

"Geez I thought that you said that we were selling in bulk. My head is heavier than that. When I think of bulk, I think of hundreds of pounds or something. Three kilograms? What is that like two pounds? Why do you need two people to carry two pounds?" I complained.

"You have no clue what you're talking about, do you?" Natalie asked. "Anyways, we are selling in bulk to these guys so that they can do whatever they want with it. They can sell it or use it. We don't really care what they do with it. We just know that they want it badly from us," Natalie continued. I sat back in my seat.

"So is this kind of drug dealing that is going on in my home town?" I asked. Natalie then turned onto the highway.

"Oh, we aren't selling in your town," Natalie explained.

"Oh really? Where are we selling?" I asked.

"Indiana," Natalie answered. My hometown was in mid-Michigan. I was sure that the drive would take at least three hours.

"Why the fuck are we going to Indiana? Can't we just sell to someone in Michigan?" I complained.

"Oh no, that would be too easy," Natalie smiled at my complaint. "Why? Do you have a job that you need to go to today?"

"Wow, you're really aiming below the belt aren't you?" I asked.

"You might as well get comfortable. It's going to be a long drive," she advised. So I did. The car seat was more comfortable than that slab of stone that the motel called a mattress. Also, it was a hell of a lot more comfortable than sleeping on a slide. So I laid my head down, shut my eyes, and fell asleep. This all seemed like a shady situation, but what other options did I have? I had nothing going for me at that point, and this seemed to be my only option. In my dreams, I dreamed of my old job. I dreamed of my old apartment. I dreamed of that Christmas. Most importantly, I dreamed of Chelsea. I dreamed of her smile, and it made me feel warm inside.

That was when suddenly my body jerked forward and my head slammed into the dashboard.

"Fucking women drivers!" I exclaimed.

"This jackass in front of me stopped short!" Natalie yelled. "Move it asshole!" She honked her horn.

"You've got a little road rage in you, don't you?" I chuckled, feeling around for a bump on my head.

"I wouldn't have road rage if they didn't give the mentally handicapped licenses!" She yelled, honking her horn.

I took a look at our surroundings. I saw that the sun was higher in the sky than when I fell asleep. I saw that we were not on the highway anymore. I also noticed that it had begun to snow while I was asleep. I scraped the boogers out of my crusty eyes, and looked up at Natalie.

"How long was I out for?" I asked.

"About three and a half hours," Natalie answered.

"Are we almost there?" I asked.

"Yeah. We're actually really close to where the other car is," Natalie explained. The car ahead of us started moving. "Fucking finally."

We ended up driving into the parking lot behind some shitty farm. There was this huge parking lot in the middle of absolutly nowhere. It seemed like it had no business being there. I mean it when I tell you that this parking lot was massive. You would expect a freaking sports stadium to be in this parking lot, but instead there was just a dinky little farm on the outside of it.

"What is this parking lot here for?" I asked.

"In the spring and summer they have the county fair," Natalie explained. "It looks really nice I hear. But since it is winter, we are taking advantage of the fact that it is desolate."

Natalie ended up parking right next to a dark blue car. It also looked like a car that my grandfather would drive. We both got out of the black car, and hopped into the blue one. She apparently had the key to the blue one. The next thing I knew, we were driving again. This time the drive only took about a half hour. That was when we finally made it to our destination. Natalie pulled into a junkyard that was absolutely desolate. There was snow everywhere. It seemed like there was barely even two inches of it, but the people apparently decided to stay inside because I saw no one anywhere. The only sign of life that I saw in the junkyard was a car with its lights on.

"Okay I need you to do this for me." Natalie looked at me with a very serious look.

"What is it?" I asked.

"Remember that we are dealing with criminals," She said. She reached over to the glove compartment and withdrew two holsters that contained pistols.

"What the fuck?" I asked.

"You are not going to touch this. Understand?" She asked. I nodded. "Just attach it to your side. This is only to look threatening. Just stand there with your arms crossed and do, not, say, a, word. Understand?" Again I nodded. "I will do all of the talking. You just stand there with your arms crossed. Look mad. Look scary. But do not talk unless I tell you to. Most likely, I will not ask you to talk. Okay?"

"I, I've never held a gun before," I admitted. I was terrified of guns. I am still terrified of guns. But hell, this was what the job entailed. Natalie effortlessly attached the holster to her hip as if she had done it a thousand times before. I could not figure out how to do it for the life of me. I couldn't tell if I had to attach it like a belt, or if I had to tie anything. "Natalie?"

"Fine," Natalie reached over and attached it to my pants for me. "It's like I'm tying a toddler's shoes."

She popped the trunk open, and we hopped out of the car. Natalie walked around the car to the trunk. She withdrew a suitcase. I followed her like a shadow. She clearly knew what she was doing. Meanwhile, I didn't. She walked halfway between our car and the other car. She then stopped, and stood there. I did the same. Then, three men emerged from the car. They all looked angry and threatening. I tried my best to look threatening as well, but I am scrawny. So I'm pretty sure that I was about as threatening to them as a puppy. All three of them had pistols attached to their sides. My heart was going a thousand miles an hour. It may have been freezing, but I was sweating bullets. The men stood in a triangle formation. One of the guys in the back had a suitcase, and the other one in the back had a scale. The one in the front spoke.

"You got what we want right?" The man asked. His voice was deep. It was more like a growl than a person's speech. Natalie lifted her suitcase.

"Three kilograms," she answered. The man in the front extended his hand, and Natalie surrendered the suitcase to him. He opened the suitcase, and removed three large plastic bags. He handed them to the man holding a scale. The two men were making sure that there were in fact three kilograms in the packages. After a few moments, which felt like hours, the two men looked at each other and smiled.

"Well it looks like you just made my day," he smiled. The man in the back with the suitcase handed his to Natalie. The other men placed the plastic bags of white powder into the suitcase and closed it.

"Can I trust that this is the right amount?" Natalie asked.

"You have our word," the man in the front answered.

"My employer does not like liars. Trust is an important thing to him," Natalie pressed.

"Believe me when I say that I don't want to anger your employer," he assured. "I had to have counted that money about five times before I was sure that it was the right amount."

"So I have your word?" Natalie asked.

"You have my word," the man answered. Then, the men retreated back to their cars. Natalie and I went back to our car. She deposited the suitcase into the trunk, and closed it. Then, we stepped back into our car. We both put our guns back into the glove compartment. After the men drove away, I spoke.

"So we drove four hours for that? Selling three kilograms of this stuff? How much money is that? Two thousand dollars? Three thousand?" I asked. Natalie laughed.

"You really are new to this aren't you?" She asked.

"Oh would you quit laughing and tell me how much money is in there?" I begged.

"There is three hundred thousand dollars in our trunk," Natalie revealed. My jaw hit the floor. My palm slammed into my forehead.

"What the absolute fuck?" I awed.

"All of it is going to our employer. He is a very wealthy man," Natalie explained.

"Oh my God," I melted into the car seat. "Three hundred thousand dollars? I've never even seen that much money, and now it's in the trunk of this car?"

"That is a good hall. I'm happy with what was made today," She turned the car on and began pulling out of the junkyard.

"How much money is usually swapped in one of those exchanges?" I asked.

"Today was a pretty average day," Natalie explained,

pulling into the street. "The highest amount that I have ever dealt with was 1.2 million."

"M-m-m-million?!" I gasped. "God damn that is so much money." That was the moment that I realized that I was so poor that the thought of a large sum of money took my breath away. It was sad really. "You could buy so much with three hundred thousand dollars. You could buy a house, you could buy three hundred thousand lottery tickets, and you could buy toilet paper for life, and you could buy a fishing boat-"

The drive home went pretty much like that. It was me drooling over money that I did not have. I had no clue who our dealer was, but I knew that he was a baller. I just knew that he had to have been living the baller lifestyle. He just had to be some hot shot who had women begging to spend just one night with him. If he made that much money in a day, how much does he make in the average year? Hell, I thought that he had a sports car nicer than any place I have ever lived. Oh my God, the thought of where a guy like that must live blew me away. He probably lives in some mansion on the coast of Lake Huron. That is what I would do.

Eventually, we made our way back to the parking lot. We swapped back into the original car that we started in. I'm sure that our employer, or someone working for him, was going to come back and pick that car up. Eventually, we made it back to the street where Stuart's tavern was.

"-and a sports car, and you could probably buy a whole restaurant, and you could buy a freaking lion. I don't know why you would want to buy a lion, but you could!" I exclaimed. Natalie parked in front of Stuart's tavern.

"As much as I would love to keep hearing what you would spend three hundred thousand dollars on, our day is over," Natalie said.

"Okay. When do I work again?" I asked.

"Same time tomorrow," Natalie answered. "Stand out here. Okay?"

"Sounds good," I replied. Natalie opened the glove compartment and removed an envelope. She handed it to me.

"Here. This is yours. Inside is payment, and a phone number. Call that number at nine o' clock sharp tonight. It is seven thirty now," Natalie instructed.

"Call this number at nine tonight. Got it," I responded. "See you tomorrow Natalie."

"See you tomorrow Kevin," She replied. So I hopped out of the car, and she drove off. I opened the envelope to see what was inside. I was in awe.

One thousand dollars in cash.

CHAPTER 6

"So were you upset?" Samuel asked.

"What do you mean upset?" Jonan asked.

"The man that you worked for had just made three hundred thousand dollars. You received one thousand. That seems like a bad deal to me," Samuel elaborated.

"You see, you are saying that from the perspective of a moderately wealthy man with a full belly and a place to live. I was a man with no money, and no place to live. The only thing that I had eaten in the past day was a hot dog. I saw a thousand dollars and all that I could think of was that I would never sleep on a slide ever again," Jonan continued. "You see my employer was smart. He knew how to hire people. He knew to hire people like me for the bullshit jobs that nobody wanted to do. If he had hired a person with a steady career to do the job that I had just done, they probably would have realized that they got a bad deal. But, a man who lived under the poverty line, who would do anything for a warm meal and a place to stay that night, would have no issues with earning a thousand dollars from that job."

I remember opening that envelope and feeling the bills in my hands. Five one hundred dollar bills, fifteen twenty dollar bills, and twenty ten dollar bills. The money was so crisp and clean that it seemed like they had just been printed it that morning. I smelled the bills, and rubbed them on my face. I looked like an idiot. I was laughing in the streets in my shitty sweat drenched suit with no underwear. I sprinted down to the nearest clothing store that I could find. I bought myself two tee shirts, two pairs of jeans, a pair of sweatpants, a jacket, four pairs of underwear, four pairs of socks, a new pair of shoes, and a backpack to hold it all in. After that, I ran back to that shitty cheap motel that I had stayed the previous night in. I got myself a room to stay the night again. After that, I went to the gas station that was right outside of the motel. There was a convenience store right next to the gas station.

The store offered were whole pizza pies for less than five dollars. So I bought one and took it to my hotel room. Those gas station pizzas are just so mediocre. The sauce was just ketchup with some pepper in it, the cheese was melted spray cheese, the crust was just stale bread, and the pepperonis had the texture of rubber. I ate all six slices. No, I didn't just eat them, I savored them. It left a greasy residue in my mouth that made my tongue stick to the roof of my mouth. I couldn't get that grease out of my mouth no matter how many bottles of water I drank.

Still, to this day, I can say that it was the greatest pizza I had ever eaten. It was shitty cardboard flavored gas station pizza. It was because I was starving. All I had consumed for the three days preceding that pizza were a hot dog, a few drinks, and cocaine. This shitty five-dollar pizza was way better than cocaine. Happiness is scarfing down a whole pizza after not eating for three days.

It's only after you hit rock bottom that you can experience true happiness.

I counted what money I had left after that spending spree. I double counted, then triple counted to make sure that I knew just how much money I had down to the last penny. It came out to seven hundred twenty-three dollars and sixty-seven cents. While working as an accountant, it had taken me a week to make five hundred seventeen dollars and sixty cents. This job earned me a thousand dollars in just a day. I was over the moon. This was easy money. This was an incredible feeling.

I then changed out of that sweaty suit. I put on underwear, sweatpants, a white tee shirt, socks, and a jacket. It was the warmest I had felt in days. I got rid of the tags and the receipt. I knew that there was no way that I was going to return any of these clothes. I laid back on the bed with the money in my hands. Just smelling the money made me happy. That was when I saw the clock.

The clock read 8:47 pm. I remembered that I needed to call the number in the envelope at nine. I thanked the heavens that my memory was jogged at that moment. I took the envelope off the dresser and put all the money back into it. Then, I removed the piece of paper with the phone number on it. This number was different from the number that I was given the previous day. It was completely different. Even the area code was changed. It seemed weird, but I accepted it. He probably had dozens of phone numbers. I pretty much stared at the clock until it hit 8:59 pm. That was when I began dialing the number onto the shitty motel land line. The phone rang once before the person on the other end answered.

"Kevin?" The man asked. His voice was deep and sinister as it had been the day before.

"Yes sir," I answered.

"How did you enjoy your work day?" He asked.

"It was fine," I answered.

"Was the payment satisfactory?" He asked. Was it satisfactory? I was jumping with joy on a street corner an hour and a half ago! Calling it 'satisfactory' was one hell of an understatement.

"Yes. I was satisfied," I stated calmly.

"Good," He responded. "Would you be interested in working for me again?"

"Yes I would," I responded.

"Excellent. Then wait outside Stuart's Tavern tomorrow again at eleven in the morning. Do not be late," he instructed.

"Will do," I answered.

"Do you have any questions for me?" he asked.

"Nope."

"Good," he then hung up.

So that was it. That was the whole conversation. He was one hell of a conversationalist. But that was it. I took a shower, put my clothes back on, and hopped into bed. I rested my head on the pillow, and went to sleep. And again,

I dreamed of Chelsea. I dreamed of her birthday the previous year. It was March sixteenth. We had her birthday party, and then a Saint Patrick's Day party the day after. There was a lot of drinking at her birthday party. It was the first time that I would cheat on her. That part of the dream made me feel like an asshole. I knew that I was an asshole, but I felt bad knowing that I hurt the one person that I cared the most about.

The next morning I woke up and paid for another night at the motel. That way I could leave my stuff in the room while I went to work. After that, I went to the gas station and bought an egg sandwich. The egg was cold and tasted like Styrofoam, and the bread was hard as a rock. It was delicious.

Then I made it to the street corner outside of Stuart's Tavern. At eleven, a car that I did not recognize pulled up in front of me. The window rolled down, and Natalie stuck her head outside of the window.

"Good morning Kevin," She greeted. I stepped inside of the car.

"What's up?" I asked. She pulled out and began driving. "So how far are we driving today?"

"It should take us about three and a half hours to get to where we need to switch cars. Then it should take another hour after that to get to our destination," Natalie explained. She sniffed the air. "Do you smell that?"

"I don't smell anything," I responded.

"Me neither. Did you take a shower?" She asked.

"Ha ha. Very funny," I responded.

"Oh, come on, you can laugh at yourself a little," She smiled. Her smiles were slight and only lasted for a second.

The majority of that trip went just like the previous trip had. Natalie and I sitting in the car and chatting for two and a half hours. The road became progressively snowier the further we drove. I assumed that we were going north. Eventually, we made our way to a large desolate parking lot with a lone car in. We swapped cars and continued on our journey. That was until Natalie drove to a park that was virtually empty except for one car with the lights off.

"Here we are," Natalie sighed. She reached over in front of me and opened the glove compartment. There again, were two guns inside of holsters. Natalie put hers on with ease. I twisted the holster in my belt loops on the jeans, but they got stuck. My face went red.

"Uh, Natalie?" I asked. I must have looked like a lost puppy.

"Again?" She chuckled.

"Yes, I know. I am pathetic," I answered. She reached around my waist and secured the holster onto my jeans. Then, we hopped out of the car. She walked around to the trunk, and removed a suitcase. The two of us then walked out in front of our car. Two men emerged from the car in front of us. They were different people from the previous day.

"You have the dope?" He had a way with greetings. He really knew how to make a person feel welcome.

"Of course," Natalie held the suitcase in the air. "You have the money that right?" One of the men smiled and held a suitcase in the air.

"Of course we have the money, just so long as you have our dope," The man explained. I stood still with my arms crossed, doing my best to look intimidating. Natalie walked closer to the men. She handed the one who wasn't talking the suitcase. That man was holding a scale. He placed the scale and the suitcase on the snow covered ground. He opened the suitcase, and removed plastic bags filled with white powder. He placed them on the scale. He looked up at the man who had done all of the talking.

"Two and a half kilograms," he spoke. The man who had talked to Natalie smiled.

"Perfect," he grinned, handing the suitcase to Natalie.

"I can trust that this is the right amount?" Natalie asked.

"What's wrong sweetheart, you don't trust me?" The man asked, lighting a cigarette.

"Answer the damn question," Natalie stammered. The man inhaled on his cigarette. "Motherfucker are you listening to me?"

"Fine, fine. Of course the right amount of money is in that suitcase. Would I really want to make an enemy out of your employer?" The man responded.

"Fine," Natalie said. She turned and began walking toward the car. I followed close behind her. She put the suitcase into the trunk of the car. We both sat inside. We sat there until the other group left. We removed our holsters and placed them into the glove compartment.

"How much money did we get today?" I asked.

"Two hundred sixty thousand dollars," she answered. My jaw dropped.

"So, are we going to be getting that kind of cash every time we work?" I asked.

"About that, yeah," Natalie answered. She put the car into drive, and we began to drive off.

"Who do we work for?" I asked. She hesitated before answering.

"You don't need that information," she answered.

"So, then why is it that all of these people seemed scared of our boss?" I asked.

"Because if they rob him and don't give him the right amount of money, our employer will ruin them," Natalie answered.

"Ruin them?" I asked.

"Our employer has hitmen that work for him. These guys are the craziest men that I ever met. They can kill you in so many different ways that it would make your head spin," Natalie continued.

"You met them?" I asked.

"I met one. He was the scariest man that I have ever met," Natalie elaborated. "His name is Lyle. I met him twice, but both times resulted in the death of somebody who wronged our employer. Our employer loves Lyle. The two of them have been working together for a long time."

"So Lyle is a hitman?" I asked.

"He is more than just a hitman. After meeting Lyle, I was convinced that I had met the devil himself. He is a stone cold man. When he kills people, he doesn't even flinch. I have no clue how many people he has killed, but I don't even think that I would want to know," Natalie explained. "I think that he enjoys killing people."

"Well I hope that I never meet this psychopath," I responded.

"You won't. I am sure that you won't," Natalie promised.

We continued on our way until we made it back to the desolate parking lot with only one car. We swapped cars again, and drove off.

"Why didn't you have a tie on yesterday?" Natalie asked.

"What do you mean?" I responded.

"Yesterday, you were wearing a suit, but not a tie. Why was that?" Natalie asked.

"I don't know how to tie a tie," I responded. She nodded.

"So I see that you didn't shave," Natalie commented.

"Yeah, I don't plan on shaving," I answered.

"Why is that?" Natalie asked.

"I like the beard."

"It would make our employer very happy."

"Well that really is a shame."

The two of us chatted for the rest of the drive. I got to know Natalie rather well. We had good conversations. It was nice to have a companion. But eventually, we made our way back to Stuart's Tavern. She handed me an envelope.

"I'll see you tomorrow," she said.

"See you tomorrow," I answered.

"There is a phone number in that envelope. Call the number at nine tonight," she advised.

"Got it," I closed the door, and she drove off. The envelope again held one thousand dollars. I made sure that Natalie was out of my line of sight. Then, on that street corner, I exclaimed "Fuck yes!" which attracted stares from all around me. I walked back to the motel building. I bought myself another pizza from the gas station. I brought it to my room, and I ate two slices. I looked at the time. It was eight thirty. Suddenly, there was a knock at my door.

I walked over to the door and opened it. There stood two muscular Asian men. One was larger than the other and wore a yellow tee shirt. The smaller one was wearing a red tee shirt.

"Kevin?" The one in the red shirt asked.

"Uh, yes?" I responded. These guys must have been co-workers.

"Good," the one in the red shirt smiled. The two let themselves inside the room. The one in the yellow shirt closed the door to the room and stood blocking it. "My name is Mason, and my associate here is Bill. Now Kevin, I was told to help you out today. Please sit down on the bed."

"Um, okay." So I sat down.

"Kevin, our employer has some guidelines for his workers to follow. You see, he wants all of us to blend into the crowd. He wants us to look like many other people. That way we are not easily identified. This comes easy to me, because, well, I'm Asian," Mason explained. "Are you following me so far?"

"Yes. I need to look boring, and you're Asian," I responded.

"Good man," Mason started. "Now, our employer strictly prohibits aesthetics on our bodies that we could easily identify us. These are things such as crazy hair styles, tattoos, facial hair, large birthmarks, large scars, facial hair, body defects, facial hair, and especially facial hair. Did I mention facial hair?"

"Yes. Multiple times actually," I responded.

"Good. Then you have the ability to count," Mason smiled. "So do you know what this means?"

"I could guess," I responded.

"Bill, please help him narrow down his guesses," Mason requested. Bill removed an electric razor from his back pocket.

"I am not shaving my beard," I answered.

"Kevin, you see my friend Bill here has anger management issues. Now I think that it would make Bill very, very happy if you were to shave your face, and when Bill is happy, you are happy," Mason put a hand on my shoulder. "I am just trying to help you."

Bill turned on the electric razor.

CHAPTER 7

I rubbed my hands down my bare face. It was smooth as a baby's butt. My previous flow of masculinity was now replaced with the face of a twelve-year-old. If you waxed porcelain and slid naked people covered in butter on it, then it still would not be as smooth as my face. It was disgusting. My once great beard was all over the floor. It was scattered on the tiled floor of the bathroom. It just laid there, lifeless, empty, and alone. I wanted to cry. This was, without a doubt, the worst tragedy of my life.

"You know, this has got to be the worst pizza I have ever had," Mason commented with a pizza slice in his hand. I looked out of the bathroom and into the bedroom. Mason and Bill stood there next to each other. Bill was still silent. I have to say though; he was the beefiest Asian that I have ever seen. You know how they are usually skinny and short? Well, Bill was the size of a car. Mason was muscular too, but he paled in comparison to his counterpart.

"Hey, that pizza is mine!" I snapped. Mason shrugged.

"It tastes like crap. It's all yours," Mason tossed the slice of pizza back in the box with the three untouched slices. Bite marks had removed half of the slice.

"Was it necessary to shave my face?" I asked.

"Those are the rules kiddo," Mason replied. "If I could, I'd tell you to dress differently too, but I'm not the fashion police. If you choose to dress like a homeless person, then that is a personal choice and I can't save you from yourself."

"But I am a homeless man," I replied. Mason looked surprised for a second.

"Okay then dress however you want," Mason mocked. "Now, since I am so kind and generous, you can keep that razor. Also, follow the guidelines that our employer gives you. It is in your best interest that he likes you." He pulled a twenty-dollar bill from his pocket and placed it in the pizza box on top of the slice that he had bitten. "Here is a little gift for your cooperation. Well, if I can call what you did as 'cooperation'."

"You know what? We are professionals and co-workers. So it is in my professional opinion that you are a dick," I insulted.

"It's a gift," Mason replied. "Now do you have any questions for me?"

"Can you do me a favor and kiss my-"

"I'll take that as a 'no'," Mason interrupted. "Come on Bill, we are leaving." Mason and Bill opened the door and began walking down the hall. "I'll see you next time you fuck up."

As they walked down the hallway, I called out to them.

"Hey! If you're crossing the street and you see the headlights of a car coming your way, do the world a favor and let that car scrape your brain across the pavement!" Neither of them even turned around to look at me when I made that comment. They just continued down the hallway. So, I walked back inside of the room and closed the door.

That had to have been to weirdest thing to happen to me. Two people just intruded on where I was staying, ate my pizza, forced me to shave, gave me a razor, and gave me a twenty-dollar bill. Obviously, I took the money. But that was just so weird. The big one did not speak once, and Mason was a dick. Also, a strange thing was that they left at exactly 8:55. That meant that I had only minutes to call my boss. But one question in my head was unavoidable; how did they know where I was? Was somebody following me here?

At nine, I called the number in the envelope. The phone rang for only a moment before my employer answered the phone.

"So were Mason and Bill gentle on you?" He asked. *Hello to you too.*

"Yes they were," I responded. "Why did I need to shave my beard?"

"In the position that you are in, I need for you to be as unmemorable as possible to our clients. If you look like a hundred other people, then there is a one percent chance of them pointing you out among other people. If you look like a thousand other people, the chance is lowered significantly. Do you understand Kevin?" He asked.

"Yes."

"Good."

"How did they know where I live?" I asked.

"I have a lot of information on you Kevin, but this is to keep you safe," he replied. I definitely did not feel safe. "People often feel safe if they don't stand out. They can blend in with the crowd. That is what I need my lower ranking employees to do."

"I understand," I responded.

"Good," He said. "Meet Natalie at eleven tomorrow outside of the gas station near your motel room."

"Will do," I agreed.

The next day, I met with Natalie at eleven right where he had instructed me to, just near the gas station outside my motel room. A bland looking car the color of sand pulled up in front of me, and the window rolled down to reveal Natalie.

"Damn, I thought I was working with an adult. You look like a man-child," Natalie joked. I stepped into the car.

"Real funny. I suffered the death of a loved one last night," I sighed. "My facial hair."

"You look like a lesbian who is trying to make herself look manly," Natalie commented.

"You look like a who from Whoville," I shot back.

"I don't want my wallet to be in the glove compartment. I'm afraid of the bugs getting in it. Can you do me a favor and put it in your purse?" Natalie asked.

"Oh, I almost forgot! I bought a gift for you. It's in my

pocket. Hold on." I reached into my pocket. I pulled my hand out of my pocket with the middle finger raised.

"Someone is cranky today. Is it that time of the month for you?" Natalie roasted.

"You can make jokes all you want," I pouted. Natalie burst into laughter. It only lasted about five seconds, but it was the first time I had heard her laugh and smile for more than a second. She just loved making fun of me. Her laugh was cute and reminded me of kittens. Her smile revealed these tiny hamster teeth. I couldn't help but smile back. For a moment, we just made eye contact while smiling without saying a word.

"So you had begun making more and more money?" Samuel asked.

"Yes. I kept collecting money every day that I worked. I worked six days a week because I had nothing else to do. I was making about six thousand dollars a week for the next four months. I calculated that, and if I kept up that pattern, I would have made over three hundred thousand dollars by the end of the year," Jonan elaborated.

"So you were making easy money?" Samuel pressed.

"Calling it 'easy money' would be an understatement. I sat inside of a car for eight hours a day and I made six figures. It was basically charity," Jonan answered.

"Now what confuses me is that you are admitting to me that you sold cocaine multiple times. You are telling a cop this information and you seem like you have absolutely no problem with it. Why?" Samuel asked.

"Officer, what would make me seem worse? Being an accomplice to selling cocaine? Or shooting two cops in the back of the head? I think I'd rather look like a burnout than a murderer. I told you at the beginning that I am not a murderer, and I told the truth," Jonan stated.

"Do you know Natalie's real name?" Samuel asked.

"You are getting ahead of yourself officer. That part comes later in the story. I wouldn't want to spoil the ending for you now would I?" Jonan smiled.

"Boy, I am not playing around. Excuse me for spoiling how this story ends for you. If you do not give me the information that I am asking for, you will end up spending a lifetime in a jail cell. There are dozens of hungry wolves in this building who want to see your head on a pike right now. I am the only thing standing in their way. So, maybe it would be in your best interest to answer my questions." Samuel instructed.

For a moment, Samuel just stared at Jonan while Jonan stared at his hands, and the handcuffs that bound him to the table.

"You still haven't told me how you got the scar on your chee-"

"God dammit boy. Do you have any brain left in that head? Or have you done so much cocaine that you sniffed your brain up just to get a high?" Samuel yelled after slamming his hand on the table. He stood up and fired bullets at Jonan with his stare.

"My elementary school teacher once said something to me that has stuck with me for my whole life. That quote is something that I think that you should hear right now Officer," Jonan looked up from his hands and at Samuel's face. "Please save all questions for the end of the presentation."

"You must think that I am either stupid, or evil," Samuel accused.

"I have met many people who have done bad things, but I am convinced that I have only met two evil men in my life, Officer."

"Alright, I'll play your game. I have met many smart men in my life, but the smartest man I have ever met once told me something that I think that you need to hear right now. Here is a quote for you boy," Samuel began. "If one looks for evil in places that it does not exist, he will trick himself into believing that he has found it."

"Now how does that apply to me?" Jonan asked.

"I am not evil. I am only here to help you. But I cannot help you if you do not give me the information that I need to help you. So please help me help you," Samuel slowly sat back down, but he never moved his gaze away from Jonan's.

"I will tell you every detail of this story I promise. I will answer every question that you have. But I need for you to be patient. Can you do that for me?" Jonan asked.

"Sure."

■■

For the rest of January, that was how my weeks went. Six days a week I would go with Natalie on a long car ride. Then I'd get back to Stewart's tavern, get my cash, and then call my employer. I also shaved daily. By the end of January, I had accumulated a good amount of money. I had so much money that I didn't know where to put it all. I managed to stuff it all inside of my backpack. I would always take my change and give it to the homeless people, because I didn't need that change. I was making six thousand dollars a week, and knew what it was like to have to sleep on a slide. If God didn't love the homeless, then I would. Also, all that I spent my money on was shitty gas station food, and that motel room.

I had purchased the same motel room throughout all of January. I spent so many nights there that it felt like home. I began to memorize all of the little quirks about it. The number three button on the controller didn't work. The window always had a gap between the window sill and the actual window. This made a constant draft. The lamp on the nightstand flickered about twice every ten minutes. I had to tolerate these little quirks, but eventually I grew to like them. It made the place have its own personality. It felt like home.

As much as I grew to love that shitty motel room, eventually I came to the realization that I needed to get a place of my own. I needed an apartment. I went around looking at cheap apartments. I got every flyer and brochure that I could find for apartments. I sat in my motel room looking at all of these newspaper ads, flyers, brochures, and pictures of apartment buildings and the price of the apartments. I felt like the motel room was judging me. It felt like I was cheating on my motel room.

But then, there was a knocking on my door. I went to open the door, and there was Mason and Bill again.

"Miss me yet Kevin?" Mason asked. I sighed.

"Are you letting yourselves in?" I asked.

"You guessed it," Mason and Bill walked right on into my room and closed the door behind them.

"I'm sorry that I don't have any pizza for you guys today," I commented.

"Kevin, we aren't here to eat your shitty gas station pizza. Do you remember what I am?" Mason asked.

"A dick?" I asked.

"I am a life coach. I am here to help you to not get caught as a drug dealer. I hear that drug dealers have a bad reputation around these parts, and by the authorities. Do you understand what I am saying?" Mason asked.

"Can you please stop beating around the bush this time and just get to the point?" I asked.

"I just love the sound of my own voice Kevin," Mason replied.

"Well I don't," I responded.

"Can't you just let me have my moment?" Mason asked. "Now, as I was saying; as far as the grid goes, you are unemployed. This means that it would look suspicious if you were to, oh I don't know, rent an apartment."

"How do you know that I am considering renting an apartment?" I asked.

"I know a lot of things. What are you thinking? What do you think people around you will think if they see you renting an apartment with no source of income? You can't just tell people that you sell cocaine Kevin," Mason stated.

"So, are you telling me that I can't rent an apartment?" I asked.

"Of course not. I am telling you that you need a legal source of income. You need a real job, along with this job," Mason continued. Bill handed me a folder with papers in it. "Here is an application for a legal tech support job. It is a bullshit easy job. We have guys in this company who are involved in the hiring process, so you are guaranteed to work there. You will work there two days a week, then work with Natalie four days a week. Then you get one day to spend by yourself. Do you understand?"

"How much does this tech support job pay?" I asked.

"The pay is shit, but you'll deal with it," Mason answered.

"But then I won't be making as much money as I do now," I stammered.

"It's either you make less money, or no money at all. Your call."

That was when Mason and Bill left. So I ended up applying to this tech support job. I was dreading it, but it ended up being the most fun job ever. All I did was sympathize with someone's issues, then redirect them to another department. It was so funny to hear the customers get pissed about their slow internet. I worked there for months and I helped absolutely nobody. It was such a fulfilling job.

CHAPTER 8

You get to learn a lot about a person from being forced to be in a car with them for hours every day. There is only so much napping and awkward silences that you can have before someone feels the need to have a conversation. Thank God we started talking. Otherwise, those car rides would have driven me mad. Maybe it was because we got along, or the fact that neither of us could stand the fact that "How Do I Live" was apparently the only God damn song that the radio station's thought existed, but we ended up talking constantly. I enjoyed spending the whole day with her. She was the closest thing that I had to a friend at the time.

One thing that I noticed was that she hugged the speed limit constantly. That was most likely because we were going to sell cocaine, and speaking to a cop was probably the worst case scenario for us. A more evident trait of hers was her apparent road rage. It was honestly hilarious.

"Okay Kevin, here is a driving lesson for you," she began. "There are a few types of people who absolutely suck at driving. I hate seeing them everywhere I go."

"Let me guess, Asian people and women," I guessed.

"You see, that is a very common misconception. Asian people are actually better drivers than most other people. They always get made fun of, so they feel like they have something to prove," Natalie responded. "Now you see, Jewish women treat every drive as if it was their first, because they don't seem like they have a fucking clue about what they're doing. They will go fifteen below the speed limit, forget that they left their blinker on, and then complain about other people on the road. But, they aren't as bad as the black guys. You see, black guys are the opposite of Jewish women. They think that they rule the whole goddam road. They think that they are so great at driving, so they speed, duck in and out of lanes, tail gate, then act like it's your fault if you get into an accident with them. That leads me to teenagers. Teenagers have the driving abilities of Jewish women, but the cockiness of black guys. Teenage boys will speed and think that they are badasses. Teenage girls will drive as terribly as Jewish women, but they understand that they suck. The worst part is that they show no effort to improve!"

"I'm confused," Samuel interrupted.

"On what?" Jonan asked.

"What does this have to do with the death of two police officers?" Samuel pressed.

Jonan started laughing. "Absolutely nothing! It's just funny!" Jonan exclaimed. Samuel glared at him.

"Boy, do I look like I find an insult to my driving skills funny?" Samuel demanded.

"Like I said officer, you should smile more," Jonan advised.

"Get on with it!" Samuel demanded. Jonan raised his hands in submission.

"Alright, alright."

....

It was February thirteenth 1998 when I got my apartment. It was a small one-bedroom apartment with a kitchen and a bathroom. There was a television in the bedroom which I liked. The kitchen was small too, but I was okay with that. At this point in time, I had stacks of money that until that point I had kept in my backpack. Now, I had a whole apartment to hide it in. Most of my money had been acquired illegally, so putting it in a bank was the dumbest thing that I could've done. So I bought a few T.V. dinners, and removed them from the boxes. Then, I put the money in the boxes, then put them back in the freezer. Sure, it wasn't the best hiding spot, but it was the first one that I thought of so I went with it. The money filled up two whole boxes.

The rest of the kitchen was a bland white color. I was okay with it. I didn't need anything fancy. I didn't even plan on spending too much time in the apartment. It was just a place for me to shit, eat, and sleep. I spent most of my time in the car with Natalie. A weird thing about that apartment was that I needed to give my new address to Mason. When he asked, I gave him a sarcastic response before I actually gave it to him. I did not argue, but I did not like giving it to him. Now, he could stop by whenever he wanted to. I'm sure that he would only show up when he had to, seeing that he didn't seem like my number one fan.

That night I laid in bed until I fell asleep. Surprise,

surprise, that night I dreamt of Chelsea.

The next day I met Natalie in front of Stewart's Tavern to go on a ride for work.

"Happy Valentine's Day," she greeted, handing me a chocolate bar.

"Oh thank you," I smiled.

"No problem! I thought it'd be fun to give a co-worker something for Valentine's Day," She explained as she started driving away.

"I didn't get you anything. I didn't know that-"

"Oh don't sweat it," she stated. I looked down at the chocolate bar and unwrapped it.

"We'll split it," I responded.

"Oh we don't have-" her sentence was interrupted by me shoving a piece of chocolate into her mouth. She swatted my hand away. "Kevin I'm driving!"

"Eat it!" I laughed.

"Kevin I'm-" She laughed.

"The power of chocolate compels you!" I exclaimed. She finally accepted it and ate the chocolate.

She smiled while chewing. When she was done, she spoke. "Wow, I bought you that? That was terrible. I am sorry I bought an off brand."

"No it's fine. I like it," I responded while taking a bite. "So what's the deal with you?"

"What do you mean?" She responded.

"Why are you working on Valentine's Day?" I asked.

"Because I was asked to," Natalie answered.

"No that's not what I was asking," I corrected, licking a brown smear of chocolate off of my thumb.

"There isn't someone at home you'd rather be with right now?"

"Oh God no," Natalie answered. "I haven't been with a man in two years."

"Really?" I asked. "Why is that?"

"That is none of your business Kevin," Natalie snapped. "Okay, why are you at work today?"

"Um…" I stuttered. I couldn't tell her why I was alone. Cheating on someone with their sister isn't exactly a great place to begin a conversation. "Alright let's talk about something else."

The rest of that day went as normal. We drove for hours and hours until we reached some desolate location to switch cars. Then we drove that car for about a half hour until we got to the people who we were selling drugs too. The whole ride though, I couldn't stop thinking about Chelsea. This Valentine's Day was supposed to be fun. Chelsea and I had been planning things to do on this day. We used to spitball ideas about various fun places that we could go. I usually did not like the ideas that Chelsea had. She would recommend dumb things like go to see a play, or take a trip to New York City, or go to an arboretum, or go to a zoo. I hated all of those ideas, but I smiled during all of those conversations. I smiled because I knew that going to those places would make her happy. If she was happy, she would be smiling, and if I got to see her smile, then I would be happy too. That's the weird thing about being in love.

I stared out the window of that car remembering so many things about Chelsea. I need to be honest with you, it hurt. It's strange to think of how one day someone loves you more than life itself, then the next they never want to see your face again. It was all my own doing. I brought this all on myself. I knew it at the time too. I hated myself. It had to have been the quietest car ride in my whole career with Natalie. Neither of us spoke up. The only noise made between us until we arrived at the spot where we had to switch cars, was a simultaneous groan when "You Were Meant for Me" came on the radio. This was followed by both of us jumping to change the station.

When we swapped cars, neither of us spoke still. Finally, we made our way to the location where the trade would take place. I opened the glove compartment, and removed two holsters with pistols inside of them. Natalie put hers on with ease. I tried to put mine on, but failed.

"You still can't put these things on?" Natalie asked.

"I'm sorry," I laughed. She reached around my waist and secured the strap for me. We stepped out of the car, and made the exchange with these strangers just like we normally would. We had done this a few dozen times together already, so I knew the routine. We got our money, they got their dope, and then we both went home. Everything went swimmingly as expected. They drove off, and then we drove off. We got back to the original car, and then began our journey back home. It seemed like it was going to be a silent ride back home again. I couldn't take another five hours of silence. I began chuckling.

"What's so funny?" Natalie asked.

"You wanna hear why I'm single today?" I offered.

"Sure," Natalie responded.

"I was dating this girl for over a year. On New Year's Eve, I made a stupid decision when I was drunk. I had sex with my girlfriend's sister. The next morning, she found out and broke up with me," I laughed.

"Why are you laughing?" Natalie asked.

"Because turning serious things into jokes helps me cope," I answered laughing. "So I am sure that no matter how bad you think your story is, it doesn't top my level of stupidity."

"Well, I guess that the reason I am single and the reason that you are single is not so different," Natalie admitted.

"Really? How?" I asked.

"I made a really dumb decision when I was drunk," Natalie answered.

"Oh my God," I laughed. "We are both piece of shit cheaters!"

"I met Brian when we were both in college. We ended up dating for four years," She began.

"Then you got drunk and cheated on him?" I chuckled. "Yup, we are the same."

"On Valentine's Day two years ago we went out to this fancy restaurant. We had a few drinks. He had more than I did, so he let me drive," she continued. I smiled in anticipation.

"So then you got home and boned his neighbor?" I continued with my comedic one liners.

"On the way home I veered off the road and wrapped the car around a tree."

Silence. I heard silence after that. Silence from me, silence from the radio, silence from her, and nothing outside to make noise. I only heard the sound of the tires against the pavement as the car moved. A tear rolled down her cheek.

"The last thing that he said was 'can you turn down the damn radio'. So I reached to turn it off, and that was the last thing that I remember..." She continued. "The doctors said that it was a miracle that I made it out with only a concussion, a few scrapes, and bruising. If the car had moved over just a few degrees to the left or to the right, I would be dead. They told me that I was lucky," Her words started to get caught in her throat. Tears continued to roll down her cheek. "Oh how lucky I was to have killed my boyfriend. I was the luckiest person in the world. What an absolute miracle."

That was followed by another moment of silence.

"I looked through his stuff in our apartment before I moved out of there a few weeks later. Hidden inside one of his suitcases was a tiny black leather box with a ring inside of it. I wanted to know what his plans were with it, but his friends wouldn't even talk to me because..." She stopped. She pulled the car over to the side of the road and put it in park. "…they thought that I was the monster who killed their friend."

She rested her head against my shoulder, and pressed her face into my chest. I heard her sobbing and wheezing out loud. I wrapped my arms around her body and held her close to me.

CHAPTER 9

"Now I appreciate you telling me that heartfelt story boy, but there is something that I am having difficulty wrapping my head around," Samuel began. "How does this story help me get to the deaths of two police officers?" Jonan began laughing. "Is something funny to you?"

"Look man I don't mean to take what you've learned as an officer and demean it, but you have no concept of the man that I worked for. You see, the significance of that story isn't just that I gained a greater bond with Natalie. That was a story that you needed to read between the lines to understand it. You see I had thought about it for a while and the death of her boyfriend had taken place on February 14th 1996. From what I understood from getting to know her is that she had begun working for our employer in April of 1996. So that means two months after her boyfriend died, she began working for our employer. Do you get what I am saying?"

"Yes," Samuel sat higher up in his seat. His eyes widened. "Okay, so a distraught woman who believes that she just killed her future husband lost many of her friends, and up rooted her whole life. Then, this man comes in two months later, while she is still impressionable. He tells her that she can have a high paying job that is easy and quick. So, obviously, she sees this as her big break and a way to reinvent her life."

"Exactly! Now what else do you notice?" Jonan asked.

"It's very similar to how you got involved with that lifestyle," Samuel admitted. Jonan began clapping with a huge smile on his face.

"So that is how this sociopath takes advantage of people. He finds them in their time of need and then hooks them in like that!" Jonan exclaimed. "If I wasn't handcuffed to this table I would high five you!"

"Did your employer have a name?" Samuel asked.

"Just another dumb pseudonym like everybody else did," Jonan replied.

"If he has a street name, then I can use that to help identify this person," Samuel persuaded. "There might have been another case involving this guy that included his street name. We could use that to help us find him."

Jonan began laughing. "No. There are no other cases involving this guy's name."

"Why do you believe that there aren't?" Samuel asked.

"Two reasons. One, his street name is so stupidly unbelievable that you wouldn't even take me seriously if I told you. Two, any person who is stupid enough to go to the police with this information would be dead before they get there," Jonan explained.

"Oh come on now why do you believe that?" Samuel asked. "You're here aren't you?"

"I can't explain my second point any further until I tell you a few more stories. Also, my first point still stands. His street name is so fucking stupid that you wouldn't believe me." Jonan repeated.

"I can only help you as much as you help me," Samuel explained.

"Fine," Jonan caved. "I wasn't even allowed to know this until early March, so I had been working with them for a few months by then."

"Alright just spit it out boy."

Jonan looked back and forth throughout the room. His eyes darted everywhere and studied the whole room before he spoke again.

"The dealer," he whispered.

"Oh fuck you," Samuel replied.

"Don't fuck me! Fuck you!" Jonan yelled. His forehead wrinkled and his eyebrows crossed.

"You honestly expect that story to hold up? That is the most generic street name I have ever heard!" Samuel belted.

"That is the beauty in it! Don't you get it! This guy is a fucking genius! He doesn't want to get caught! I never saw him in person, so I don't even know what he looks like! He probably altered his voice on those phone calls! And his name is so goddam stupid that no cop in their right mind would believe a thug who gave them that story! Don't you see that this guy is so manipulative that even his name is bringing us to an argument?" Jonan pleaded.

Samuel looked Jonan in the eye. "I am warning you boy. I am going to pay close attention to every detail of your story. I will blow any holes that I see in it wide fucking open.Do you understand me?" Samuel stammered, pointing his finger at Jonan.

"I promised you that I would never lie to you," Jonan answered. "Can I continue with my story?"

. . . .

Let me explain something about Saint Patrick's Day. It sucked. I dreamed about Chelsea that entire night. I woke up the next day with nothing to do. So I did what any other sad and lonely person does on Saint Patrick's Day. I drank. I drank so much that Mel Gibson would have told me to slow down. Anyway, my point is that nothing good happened on March 17th 1998.

So, on March 18th, I went on a job with Natalie. I was completely hungover.

"God dammit Kevin, you look like shit," she exclaimed.

"Now you have a talent for greetings. Really, you do," I replied.

"You smell like an alcoholic stepdad burped," she said.

"Wow, that was an oddly specific insult," I replied.

"Like, really. You smell like someone left a sponge in a jar of moonshine for ten years," Natalie continued.

"Okay you aren't done I guess."

"You smell like a sweaty drunk took a piss on an even sweatier drunk," she laughed. Then, she just giggled for about half a minute straight. Ten seconds into it, I began laughing with her. When the laughing ended, we were just looking into each other's eyes smiling for a few seconds. "We should get going." So she put the car in drive, and we were off.

That evening was different than our usual work days. Our conversation did not stop for hours while we were driving. During that time, neither of us ran out of stuff to talk about. We made fun of those shitty pop songs on the radio. We talked about our favorite music, we talked about our families, and we were laughing for most of the conversations. I learned a lot about her that day. I learned that her favorite movie was "The Lion King", her favorite song was "Life in the Fast Lane" by the Eagles, her favorite color was yellow because of sunrises, her mother was a doctor, and so many other things. Whenever we stopped at a red light, she turned to look at me while we were talking.

We eventually reached some desolate parking lot with a lone car for us to use. We switched into that car, and took off again. I was almost disappointed when we reached our destination. It was someplace south, because it was much warmer than where I lived. We were in some sandy junkyard out in the middle of nowhere. There were trash bags everywhere, abandoned rusty cars with missing windows and wheels, broken pieces of guitars, tables without legs, legs without tables, and a smell so bad that my terrible smell was barely noticeable. Natalie parked near one of the rusty cars.

I attempted to strap the gun holster to my waist, and failed.

"Oh come on Kevin. You've been doing this for almost three months," Natalie complained, but still smiled at me.

"I just can't do it man," I replied. She reached her arms around my waist to strap the holster to my belt loops. Then she looked up at me and looked into my eyes when she finished.

"There you go," she smiled, lightly tapping my cheek. "Now you look good."

"I didn't before?" I chuckled.

"Maybe," she smirked. She put on her sunglasses and hopped out of the car. I put on my sunglasses, and we went to work. We walked behind the car, and Natalie opened up the trunk. She pulled a suitcase from the trunk, and then shut it. We both walked in front of the car and awaited whoever was in the car across the junkyard.

He stepped out of his car, looking like a mess. He was wearing a bathrobe that hung open, revealing a wife-beater and boxers. Natalie and I gave each other a look that spoke louder than any words we could use to make fun of this guy. His hair was some mix of a faded blonde and orange. His teeth were stained yellow. Nothing about his appearance led me to believe that he was a successful person at all. He was buying expensive cocaine, so I was sure that he just looked like a homeless person. He had a silver suitcase in his left hand that was identical to our suitcase, and a scale in his right hand.

"Hey fellas!" He cheered. "You guys got the stuff?"

"That suitcase has our money right?" Natalie asked.

"Of course it does honey," he smiled, knocking on the

suitcase. He was not at all like the other previous customers. He made no attempt to be threatening, and he actually seemed like he wanted to be our friends. He walked over to Natalie and I. He opened the suitcase revealing stacks and stacks of money. "You want to count it?"

"We don't need to, correct?" Natalie asked.

"I would say not. I don't want to make any enemies with your boss man, and you seem like kind folks don't ya?" He smiled, closing the suitcase. He handed it to Natalie. Natalie handed him our suitcase. He unclipped the suitcase and removed the plastic bags of cocaine. He placed them on his scale, and smiled. "Two and a half kilograms. Beautiful."

"So is everything satisfactory?" Natalie asked.

"I am way more than satisfied," He cheered. He extended his arms to the side smiling. "There we go! Easy right?"

Natalie and I did not respond.

"Alrighty, I'll just go then. Have a nice day you kids," He turned and began walking towards his car. Natalie and I stayed in front of our car while he trekked to his. It seemed to be about fifty yards away. About halfway to his car, he turned back to us. "Oh, I almost forgot to tell you guys that-"

Then his head exploded with a loud bang.

CHAPTER 10

That was the first time I witnessed a man die right in front of me. A red gush shot straight up in the air and landed in the sand below him. His body fell to the side with a loud thud. Most of his head was gone. I saw a large shard of his skull flip into the air high above him, only to pierce the ground about twenty feet from his body. Natalie was screaming something at me, but I don't remember what it was. My body's reaction was to freeze up. My muscles did not permit me to move. There was another loud bang, and then metal collided with the rusted car behind me.

I didn't realize it in that moment, but I had just missed being shot in the chest.

I ducked behind the rusted car, and Natalie hid behind the wheel of our car. I started fiddling with the gun inside of my holster, but I couldn't withdraw it. I had this damn thing on my side multiple times a week over the previous two and a half months, and I never had to use it. This was my call to action, but I couldn't answer it because I couldn't withdraw my fucking gun.

I peeked above the car, to see a large man with sunglasses in a jean jacket and wife-beater. He had bright red hair, and a bright red full beard. In his hands, was a pump action shotgun that I could not identify. He was shooting at the car that I was hiding behind. I instantly ducked my head behind cover again.

Eventually, I withdrew the pistol from my holster and held it in my hands. I had never held a gun before. My fingers wrapped around the trigger like I had seen in movies. I held the gun above the car without poking my head up so that my head wasn't exposed. I aimed in the general direction that I believed the man was in. Then, I pulled the trigger. Unfortunately, it wouldn't click. That was when I remembered that I must have left the safety on. I brought the gun back behind cover again, and desperately looked for the safety button. I was looking for a bright red switch on the side of the barrel, but I quickly realized that it was the bright red button with a black top on the side of the trigger.

My focus was ruined when I heard another shot come in my direction. One of the tires of the car that I was hiding behind popped.

"Stop!" I screamed in a hysterical hurry. The man did not respond to me. A bead of sweat dripped from the tip of my nose and onto the barrel of the gun. I had to re-find the safety button and push it. I heard a click, and the red was no longer visible. I had to mentally prepare myself for the fact that I either needed to kill, or be killed. I looked into the rearview mirror of the car that I hid behind, and saw the man getting closer and closer to me. I knew that I needed to act immediately.

I took a deep breath and exhaled a roar. I jumped up

with my gun and aimed at his face. That was when I heard a loud bang, and the back of his head blasted behind him. He collapsed backwards into the sand. But something was wrong. I aimed at him, but I never pulled the trigger. I turned to our car, and saw Natalie with her pistol drawn in a professional stance. She looked to me with her jaw dropped.

"Get in the car!" She yelled at me. She jumped into the front seat, and I jumped into the shotgun seat. I put the gun's safety on.

"What the fuck was that?" I demanded.

"I don't-" She began, but she stopped when she looked into the rearview mirror. Then, she quickly put the car in drive and sped off. I looked behind the car to see two other people aiming guns at us from afar. They never shot though. I guess that we were too far away for them to accurately shoot.

We drove past the nice man who was buying from us. I saw the puddle of blood that he was lying in. We got out of the junkyard and onto the main road.

"What the fuck just happened?" I screamed in a hysterical fit.

"I have no fucking idea!" She screamed back at me.

"Who was that fucking guy?" I asked.

"How the fuck would I know?" She replied. She removed her gun holster and handed it to me. "Put both of ours in the glove box now!" So I did.

"What the fuck do we do now?" I asked.

"Stop talking."

"Who were those fucking guys?"

"Stop asking me questions." She drove onto a jug handle to get onto a large bridge. Hopefully, one that would take us far away quickly.

"Where are we going?" I asked.

"Shut up. Please!"

"But I-"

"I have no idea what the fuck happened either! I am trying to figure this out so will you please just do me the one simple favor that I asked, and shut, the fuck, up!" She screamed. Then we heard the all too familiar sound of a police siren behind us. She looked into the rearview mirror and saw the flashing lights of a police cruiser behind us. "Shit!"

"What now?" I asked. She breathed heavily in annoyance.

"Please just don't say another word."

She pulled over and the cop pulled up behind her. She put the car in park. The cop stepped out of his car, and began walking toward us. Natalie rolled the window down.

"Good evening officer," she smiled. I tried to smile as well.

"License and registration please," he asked.

"Of course," Natalie responded. She removed her license and registration and gave it to the officer. He inspected them.

"Missy, do you know why I pulled you over?" He asked.

"Is my tail light out? My friends have been telling me about how I should always be checking that and I know that I should listen to them, but I'm just too stubborn sometimes. I'm not good with cars. You know how that is, your girlfriend must be that same way though right officer?" she rambled.

"I don't have a girlfriend, but thank you," he stated, handing back her license and the car's registration. "And your taillight is fine. Do you know what the speed limit is here young lady?"

"Fifty-five?" Natalie asked.

"Yes fifty-five. I caught you going fifty-eight back there," The officer continued. He lowered his sunglasses to make eye contact with her. "And aren't you too pretty to break the law young lady?"

My body loosened completely.

"Oh I'm so very sorry officer. I promise that it won't happen again," Natalie responded.

"You promise?" He asked.

"I promise," Natalie answered. The officer smiled.

"Alright sweetheart I'll let you off with a warning, but next time I'll have to give something to you," he smiled.

"It won't happen again," she promised.

"You kids enjoy your evening." He began walking

back to his car. Natalie and I remained silent until he drove off.

When he was out of sight, Natalie and I made eye contact, smiled, and simultaneously screamed "Yeah!" as we high fived. Both of us were dripping in sweat, out of breath, and red in the face. She started the car and began driving as I tried to catch my breath.

"Okay, so now what?" I asked. She sat there silently for a moment. All I heard was the wheels rotating and wind whizzing by.

"I... I don't know," Natalie answered.

"Well, where are we going?" I asked.

"I'm going to take you home," Natalie answered.

"Is that safe?" I asked. She didn't respond. "Is that safe?"

"I'm not sure," She answered. "I need to call the Dealer. Hold on." Natalie pulled her phone out from the cup holder. She pushed the buttons until it started calling. She played with the antenna at the top of the phone with her finger as it rang. "Hello sir. Something happened. We got attacked... Some guys started shooting at us when we were trying to sell, and the guy that we were selling to got shot in the head. We had to leave the briefcase of money and the briefcase of drugs there. Otherwise we would've been shot too. We saw three men but there could've been more."

Then, there was silence. The Dealer must have been talking to her. It seemed like she was getting more upset, but she was hiding it rather well.

"I killed one of them, yes," she spoke. There was silence again for a while. "Okay, I will." Then she hung up.

"What did he say?" I asked.

"Well, for starters, I am going to take you back to your apartment," she answered.

"What? Why?" I asked. "How do I know if that is safe?"

"The Dealer promised me that you'll be safe there," Natalie answered.

"How does he know that it's safe?" I asked.

"There will be guys monitoring it. You should be fine," Natalie answered.

"Should?" I asked.

"I won't sugarcoat anything for you. The Dealer is looking into it and we'll get updated as soon as we can. But for now we just need to be patient," Natalie answered. I didn't like that answer, but it was all that I could get. After sitting in silence for a few minutes, I spoke up.

"Natalie."

"Yes?" She responded.

"You saved my life today..."

"Yes I did."

"I got scared and completely choked up. I had no idea what to do in that situation, but you completely owned it."

"What are you trying to say?" She asked.

"Thank you," I gulped.

After a few hours of driving, we got back to my apartment. It was dark out and mildly raining. I was scared to leave the car. The walk across the parking lot terrified me. I looked at Natalie.

"Take the gun and holster out of the glove compartment and take it into your apartment with you," she advised. "I don't expect you to need it, but just take it."

"Thank you." I took the gun from the glove compartment.

"I think that we'll see each other tomorrow. The Dealer will call you tonight with further information," she explained. "I'll stay here and watch you go across the parking lot to the building."

"Do you want to stay the night?" I asked.

"That would not be a good idea," she answered.

"Thank you again. Good night." At that, I hopped out of the car with the gun hidden under my clothes, and ran across the parking lot and into the building. I was out of breath from the run mostly because I am out of shape. I turned around and there was a resident of the building standing right behind me. I didn't notice him when I came in, so I jumped when I turned to see him.

"Wow, you look like you just saw a ghost," he chuckled as he exited the building. I quickly rushed to my apartment. I made sure to lock the door behind me. With the gun in my hand, I looked at the safety, and turned it off. My heart was racing after looking around my apartment. The bedroom and bathroom doors were closed.

Cautiously, I stood with the pistol the same way that I had seen cops in movies hold their pistols before storming a room. I reached my hand up to the doorknob to the bedroom. I then swung the door open, and ran in with my pistol and waved it around looking for any person who may have been waiting for me. There was no one there. So, I stepped out of my bedroom, and stood before the door to the bathroom. I posed like they did in the movies, and then swung the door open the same way I did in my bedroom. Again, there was no one. But, it was possible for someone to be hiding behind the shower curtain. So, I swung it open with my pistol aimed, only to find no one.

I outwardly exhaled out of relief. I turned the safety back on the pistol, and stood there feeling safe. That was when the phone began to ring. This made me jump out of fear, which knocked the shower rod out of its socket and onto my head. I swung my arms to remove the curtain from my body. Then, I walked into the kitchen and answered the phone.

"Hello?" I answered.

"What was that goofy ass run that you made to your apartment? Man you should've seen the way that you ran. It was hilarious!" A familiar voice spoke.

"Mason?" I asked.

"Aren't you thrilled to hear from me?" Mason laughed. He sounded like he was eating. "Let me guess, you panic checked your apartment for baddies?"

"What? No I didn't," I lied.

"There was no need to, I already did it," Mason

answered.

"How did you get into my apartment?" I asked.

"Don't worry about the unnecessary details. Good ol' Bill and I are in a car outside your apartment building right now. Believe me, no one suspicious is getting into that apartment without us noticing," Mason explained. "We'll be here all night. Bill's been talking up a storm. I swear he won't shut up." Mason chuckled. I was not amused. "It's a joke asshole. You're allowed to laugh."

"So what do I do?" I asked.

"Well, at seven pm sharp tomorrow night you need to go to where you usually get picked up by Natalie. You guys are going to have a long night ahead of you. Get some sleep before then," Mason explained.

Needless to say, I got no sleep that night.

Chapter 11

Jonan locked his fingers together. A bead of sweat dripped from his hairline and rolled down his forehead to his nose. It dripped to the point of his nose, and hung from the tip. Jonan's trembling body knocked it to the handcuffs around his wrists. His face was burning red. He just sat there staring at his hands.

"I… I had never seen a person die before that day," Jonan choked. He bent his head over to his hands so that he could wipe sweat from his forehead. "That happened two weeks ago. Earlier this week I saw a man drop a porcelain cup, and… and when I saw the shard of porcelain fly away from it and hit the ground all that I could imagine was the shard of skull hitting the ground."

"Did you know the name of the man who was shot in the head?" Samuel asked.

"I don't know his name, what town I was in, or any of the names of the guys who were there. I wish I could tell you, but I can't," Jonan answered.

"You expect me to believe that you don't know any of that information?" Samuel challenged.

"You can believe me or not. I don't care. It won't make me magically know where the town is or that guy's name," Jonan answered quivering. "Can I get a break? A lunch break? I've got that fifth amendment. That lets me go on breaks right?" Jonan asked weakly. The cocky confidence of his demeanor had melted away into a weak, vulnerable one.

Samuel sighed. "Fine. You'll get forty-five minutes. Okay?" Samuel answered.

"You're a saint man," Jonan replied. Samuel turned to leave. "Wait. Hold on. Where are you going?"

"I'm getting someone to get you food," Samuel answered.

"Are you going to eat with me?" Jonan asked.

Samuel chuckled. "I'm not going to share a meal with you." Samuel walked out and shut the door. He walked throughout the building. Frank saw him and ran to him.

"Sam! Did you get him to confess yet?" Frank asked excitedly.

"Not yet," Samuel replied.

"Why the fuck not Sam? You've been in there for hours. What's the deal man?" Frank asked.

"This fucking kid has gotten himself involved with the wrong people. That's why his story is so long," Samuel answered.

"Okay whatever. I have news for you. They found three things on Casey. They found a pair of car keys, a cell phone, and an M1911 pistol," Frank informed. "The cell phone has a message saved to it from last night at six forty-five. Then, he made a phone call which ended at eight thirty-two, about a half hour before we were called to the scene. But here is where it gets weird. The pistol on him had eight rounds in it."

"What's so weird about that?" Samuel asked.

"Come on Sam. You should know this. His M1911 holds a maximum of eight bullets. If he shot a minimum of two rounds at the officers' heads, then the gun should have six bullets left. But the problem is that it had all eight. So you would think that he switched magazines right? But our problem is that the ballistic experts don't even believe that the gun has been fired in weeks, or even months," Frank explained.

"So what does that mean for us?" Samuel asked.

"It means that there is either a second gun that we haven't found yet for whatever reason, or he didn't do it. But come on, are we even going to consider that he didn't do it?"

Frank chuckled. "It's just a hole in the story that we need to fill up. But nevertheless, you need to ask him about those things."

"What was the voicemail?"

"Just some guy asking for Casey to call him back. Nothing major. There was no useful information in it. He left his radio on during the call, but it didn't tell us anything useful," Frank answered. "So you gonna go back and talk to him again?"

"He wants a lunch break," Samuel replied. Frank looked appalled.

"You're actually giving this guy a lunch break? Have you gone soft?" Frank asked.

"If I wasn't also starving myself, then I wouldn't have given it to him. Also, if I don't get a cigarette soon, I think that I might just kill a man," Samuel answered. "That reminds me, can you get that kid a sandwich?"

"I'm an officer of the law Sam. I'm not this kids fucking waiter," Frank snapped.

"Frank, just get him a damned pimento loaf sandwich. I'll be back in a half hour," Samuel demanded.

"I'm going to piss in his sandwich Sam." Frank reluctantly agreed to get the sandwich.

Samuel turned and left the building. He removed a pack of cigarettes from his pocket and a lighter. He withdrew a single cigarette from the pack. He placed the brown tip on his lips, and ignited the lighter. A puff of smoke erupted from his mouth, and he put the pack and the lighter away in his pocket. Samuel stood with the cigarette in his mouth, basking in the sun. Samuel was also hungry. So he started walking through the parking lot to his car. He stopped upon seeing something familiar; a red 1997 Ferrari. Inside, there was a familiar face. Samuel tapped on the glass to get the man's attention. From within the car, Jerry's face lit up. He opened the door and stepped out of the vehicle.

"Sammy!" Jerry greeted, hugging Samuel.

"Uncle Jerry, what are you doing in this parking lot?" Samuel asked. Jerry looked around for a moment.

"Oh I was just waiting for you. I wanted to take you out to

lunch before I left tonight," Jerry answered. He motioned to his car. "Please come in."

"I don't have a lot of time for lunch," Samuel warned.

"Oh please Sammy I insist. It might be the last time we go out to lunch for a long time," Jerry responded. Samuel thought about it.

"Sure," Samuel stepped into the vehicle. Jerry drove them to a nearby diner that had four tables filled in the whole restaurant. Samuel and Jerry sat down immediately.

"So how is your case going?" Jerry asked.

"Oh it's getting interesting," Samuel sighed.

"How so?" Jerry asked, not looking up from his menu.

"This kid got involved with people that he shouldn't have," Samuel answered. "I shouldn't say any more than that though."

"Did you know the officers who were killed last night?" Jerry asked.

Samuel looked up from his menu at Jerry. "How did you know about that?" He asked.

"Word spreads fast. Especially a story like that," Jerry answered. "Monica read about it in the newspaper and told me about it."

"What did she say?" Samuel asked.

"She was just concerned that maybe you knew one of them," Jerry continued.

"Oh, no. I only had brief conversations with one of them. I never even met the other one. That's probably the only reason that I was allowed to be on this case. I'd have the least amount of bias. Even with that, it's hard to be impartial on a case where fellow officers died. We're a big family. So, I feel for them even though I didn't know them. Do I sound crazy or do I make sense?" Samuel asked.

"Of course you don't sound crazy. I know exactly what you mean," Jerry answered. He took a sip of his water.

"So are you excited to restart your whole life?" Samuel smiled.

"Oh, of course I am," Jerry exclaimed. "I got this pamphlet detailing all of the vacuums I'll be selling. You won't believe it Sammy! Get this! There is a vacuum that revolves around a large swiveling ball, instead of wheels. So, it has a wider degree of turning than a typical vacuum. Isn't that incredible?" Jerry spoke with enthusiasm.

"You're so passionate about vacuums," Samuel laughed.

"How could I not be? These things are incredible! There is one that runs on water instead of electricity. How great is that?" Jerry smiled.

Samuel laughed even harder. "You're a natural born salesman. So let me ask you Uncle Jerry. If you are going to be a vacuum salesman, how do you plan on affording a Ferrari?" Samuel asked.

Jerry looked downward. "It's funny how you mention that..." He began. "Sammy, I'm selling the Ferrari."

Samuel's jaw dropped. "You're selling it? But that's your baby," Samuel responded.

"I know. I just can't take it with me. After I drop you off at the station I'm taking it to some guy's house to sell," Jerry explained.

"But then how will you be getting to Arizona?" Samuel asked.

"Oh my friend will be taking me," Jerry answered. "He'll be picking me up tonight. You'll probably get home from work as I'm leaving."

"Well I wish you the best of luck. Of course I want you to succeed in whatever you do," Samuel encouraged.

"Thank you for putting a roof over my head in my time of need," Jerry said.

"I'm going to miss telling my friends that the Ferrari in the driveway was mine," Samuel chuckled.

"I'm going to miss actually having the Ferrari," Jerry chuckled.

Then, the waitress walked over to them. "Have you two decided on anything to order yet?" She asked smiling.

"I'm going to get, ah, French onion soup," Jerry answered, smiling at the waitress. She wrote it down on a little sheet of paper.

"And for you?" She asked, looking at Samuel.

"I'll get a Reuben," Samuel replied, not looking up from his menu. She wrote that down too.

"Can I get you anything to drink?" She asked.

"Water," Samuel answered.

"I'll get unsweetened iced tea. Thank you," Jerry said. She wrote down both of the orders.

"Okay, I'll get you your drinks in a moment," She answered, taking the menus away.

Jerry waited for her to be gone. "You know Sammy, you really should have thanked her," Jerry advised.

"She's getting paid, she doesn't need my thanks," Samuel answered. Jerry wagged his pointer finger.

"Now Sammy, I worked at a restaurant for three years in my high school days. I remember all of the little things that waiters and waitresses appreciate customers doing. For example, saying a simple thank you," Jerry explained.

"This woman is going to see dozens of customers today. My thank you won't change a thing about her day," Samuel answered.

"When someone is fixing your car, do you thank them?" Jerry asked.

"Well of course I do," Samuel answered.

"Why is that?" Jerry questioned.

"Because I don't want them to mess with my car," Samuel replied.

"Do you want her to mess with your food?" Jerry asked.

"It's a Reuben Uncle Jerry. What could she possibly do that is so bad?" Samuel asked.

"Well, if you overstep your bounds with someone who is fixing your car, they might slash your tires. If you over step your bounds with a waitress, she might spit in your food," Jerry explained.

"Now don't you think that slashing my tires is a little bit of an overreaction?" Samuel asked. Just then, the waitress approached the table with the drinks.

"Water for you." She placed the cup of water in front of Samuel. "And an iced tea for you." She smiled at Jerry. "Your food should be out in a few minutes."

"Thank you so much," Jerry smiled. He eyed Samuel.

"Uh, thank you," Samuel stuttered.

"You're welcome," She smiled back. Then she walked

away. Jerry smiled at Samuel.

"See, that time she smiled at you and not just me," Jerry stated.

"That's all in your head," Samuel replied, sipping his water.

Chapter 12

Samuel opened the door and entered the room. Jonan still sat at the table with his hands handcuffed to the table. There was a paper plate with crumbs and a half empty water bottle in front of him.

"That guy who brought me this sandwich was a real nice guy. He said that he put vinegar on it. I swear I tasted it," Jonan said.

"Why did you have a gun on you?" Samuel asked, closing the door behind him.

"Officer, I've had a gun on me plenty of times. That question doesn't narrow anything down for me," Jonan mocked.

"Last night boy! Why did you have a gun on you last night?" Samuel demanded.

"Now you see that doesn't ring any bells," Jonan mocked.

"Boy you are not in a position to be fucking with me! I have your name. I have your ass. I have your life in my hands! So I am not the kind of person that you want to be fucking with! I gave you your damn break. Now answer my questions!" Samuel demanded.

"Officer, I told you that I will answer all of your questions. You just need to let me finish my story. If you have any further questions, then I'd be happy to answer them. Just please let me finish my story," Jonan pleaded.

"Fine. But you better hurry up," Samuel agreed, sitting down. "I'm getting tired of waiting hours just to hear nothing from you."

"Well, all that night I dreamed of Chelsea. You see, in my dream, the events of that day just kept replaying in my head over and over again. The only difference is that instead of the nice man in a robe whose skull turned into a thousand-piece puzzle, it was Chelsea's head that got shot. Weird right? I don't know if there is some psychological thing with that, but I do know that it was fucking weird. Women right?" Jonan explained. "The next day I knew that I needed to meet up with Natalie at seven at night. So I had enough time to buy a car. I went out really early to a local car dealership. I purchased a car in all cash up front. I had all of the money that I needed. It was money that had just been sitting in a freezer for months. But it was money, so they took it. I didn't get any insurance because I was afraid. I don't know what I was afraid of, but I was afraid."

"What kind of vehicle was it?" Samuel asked.

"It was a used 1992 Honda Civic. It was used. That way it was the cheapest thing that I could buy. This thing was so bland looking that anyone could easily lose it in a crowd of vehicles."

When I got back to the apartment, I parked in my parking

spot that came with the apartment. I really had never used it up until that day. It was so weird. Spending as much time in a car as I had for the past three months, had not prepared me for being in the driver's seat for the first time. I must've been driving like an asshole. I was driving ten miles below the speed limit the whole way home, and I was a nervous wreck the whole time. That also could have been because I almost died the night before. One weird thing about the car dealership was that they were advertising an event. They had given me a flier for a masquerade event at Stewart's Tavern that was planned for the following Friday night. So that brings us to last night, March 27th. The flier had these little tabs that you could pop out that turned it into a flimsy mask. It was easily one of the dumbest gimmicks that I had ever seen.

So I parked and stepped out of my car, holding the flier. A guy who I had never seen before approached me. He was a scraggly looking guy. His beard was disgustingly long. He had liver spots all over his face. He wore a wife beater and basketball shorts. On his head was a snapback. He wore a robe over his clothes, and his shoes had holes in them that revealed his toes.

"Wow, nice ride man," he greeted. I looked at him confused.

"Uh, thanks?" I responded. My car was literally garbage.

"Do you live here?" he asked.

"Um, yeah. I live in this building right here. Do you?" I asked.

"Well I guess that you could say that. I live in there." The man pointed to a car parked across the street. It was the worst looking car that I had ever seen. It made my car look like the gold standard of American automobiles. The paint was a vomit green that appeared to have been chipping off. The tire tread seemed completely worn off. Three of the windows had cracks in them. It was an absolute piece of trash.

"Nice place." I lied.

"Thanks man." He extended his hand. "I'm Randall."

"Oh, I'm Jonan," I answered, shaking his crusty hand.

"So nice to meet you Jo man. I don't meet a lot of new people," Randall sighed.

"Why's that?" I asked.

"Because some people think that I smell a little too much," Randall answered. "You wanna hear a secret?"

"Sure," I responded.

"I like my stench. It's the musk of the all-natural man, man," Randall explained. He scratched his beard and a spider crawled out of it. That's when his smell really hit my nostrils.

"Randall, I, uh, really should get inside. I've got a lot of work to do today. Sorry," I explained.

"You shouldn't be working for the man, man! That's how they brainwash you!" Randall sounded crazy. On any other day I would've told Randall off, but this day was special. I had almost died the previous night, so the acid trip known as Randall was tolerable. Somehow, I managed to escape the conversation and make my way back to my apartment. I went back inside and opened my door to see two people standing in my kitchen.

"What are you doing in here?" I asked Mason and Bill.

"We were checking it out to make sure that no one was in here who wanted to kill you," Mason answered. "I found one and his name is Mason, but I'm not going to kill you because I'm such a nice guy." Mason bit down on an apple in his hand.

"Is that my apple?" I asked.

"Of course it is," Mason answered, biting it again. "I was looking through your cabinets for food because I was hungry. Why do you have lemon chai green tea? I thought that that was only for fruits and women over fifty."

"First of all, I like it. Second of all, it's good for my cholesterol. Third of all, fuck you. Fourth of all, I can do whatever I want," I answered.

"You sound so unhappy to see me. So I see that nothing has changed," Mason chuckled. "We'll get out of your hair," Mason replied. He looked over at the gargantuan Bill. "Come on Bill we're out." Bill nodded, stood up, and walked to the front door with Mason. Mason turned to me before he left. "Alright kid just remember, seven o'clock tonight, meet Natalie where you normally meet her. This is very important, understand?"

"Yes I understand," I answered.

"Now you see Bill is really in a good mood right now, but the problem is that if you chicken out and don't go, then you will have put Bill in a bad mood, and I'd hate to see Bill in a bad mood. It wouldn't be good for either of us because then

I'm going to have to spend the whole night cleaning, and I don't particularly enjoy cleaning. So please just do the three of us a favor and show up tonight," Mason explained. Translation: if I didn't show up, I'd get beaten so hard that I'd wish that bullet had hit me in the chest.

"I get it," I answered.

"Good!" Mason clapped his hands together. "Peace loser." Bill and Mason turned and walked out of the apartment, and down the hallway. I closed the door behind them. I leaned up against the closed door, and slid down until I hit the floor. I exhaled louder than I ever had before. The time was five thirty-seven. I had an hour and twenty-three minutes until I travelled into the deep unknown. My mind ran wild with what I thought could happen. Would Natalie be okay? Was I getting into a shootout? Was I going to kill someone? Was I going to die?

I removed the pistol from the pocket on the inside of my jacket. I took it with me because I was scared to be unarmed. I flipped the safety switch from on to off over and over again just to get a feel for it. I studied the gun in my hands. I had never shot a gun before, and I never killed anyone. I wanted those two things to remain true by the end of the night, but I had no way of knowing.

I turned to get on my knees, and prayed. I was never really a religious person, but when you fear for your life, believing in God is way cozier than facing reality. The first person that I prayed for was Natalie. Next, was myself. After that were my Mom and Dad. Finally, Chelsea. I prayed for Natalie because she was the most amazing person that I had ever met, and I didn't want anything bad to happen to her. Natalie was the one person that I could not imagine spending a single day without. I thought of her all the time. I was sad to see her car drive away at the end of each day. I had grown to love so many things about her; her smile, her little teeth, the way she makes fun of me as a greeting, her road rage, us laughing together, and most of all, the way she makes me feel. I prayed for myself because I was afraid of dying. I prayed for my dad because I knew that if he were still alive he would have been disappointed in me. If he could speak to me now, he would be wise enough to tell me how to get out of this situation. I prayed for my mom because I felt guilty for not contacting her in months. She raised me and I let her down. Finally, I prayed for Chelsea because she is such a great person, who deserves to be with someone special. I was not that person. I was not special. I was a horrible boyfriend who constantly let her down, and I recognized that. I hoped nothing but the best for her. Also, I hoped that I could finally get over her.

6:57 pm.

My car rolls into the parking lot of Stewart's Tavern. I exited my vehicle and stood where I always did. This time was different. We had never gotten together at night. Every job before this one had been in the morning. Now, we were getting together at night. My fingers were twitching. Beads of sweat were dripping from my forehead. I saw the car roll in front of me. The window rolled down and there was Natalie. I stepped into the car and shut the door behind me. Natalie then began driving. She had no insulting method of greeting me this time. She was quiet. She was dead silent. I had no idea how to begin a conversation. I turned to look at her as the car moved through the streets. You could cut the tension with a knife. I had never seen Natalie like that. She did not even recognize my existence. I knew that something was up.

Something was going to happen. I had no clue what, but something was going down that night.

"Can we-"

"Please not tonight Kevin," She snapped. Her voice was trembling. "Not tonight," she whispered. The radio was silent. Neither of us spoke a word. For two hours I stared at the night sky. We drove down roads that I had never even seen before. We had driven down roads with nothing but cornfields in every direction. We drove down roads with open grasslands on both sides. There were no other cars on the road but ours'. I never thought that I would see such desolate places as I did on that car ride.

Remember how we always drove to a desolate location to swap cars? Well this time was different. Much different.

Suddenly, we were driving through a forest. We reached a part of the forest that didn't even look like it had roads anymore. The places that we usually make the car switch were parking lots with no other cars. This place was different. There wasn't even pavement anymore. We got to this opening in the trees that spanned roughly fifty feet in diameter. The only thing there other than grass, rocks, and our car was another car sitting with the lights off.

"Get out," Natalie instructed. I did not ask any questions. I made sure that the holster was secure on my hip, and then I exited the car. Like an obedient dog, I followed Natalie. We walked to the other car, but something was off. There was a person in the driver's seat. Natalie sat in the shotgun seat, and I sat in the back.

Remember how earlier I told you that I had only ever met two evil people in my life? Well, I introduce you to numero uno. I didn't know it at the time, but the man in the driver's seat was, and still is, the most terrifying man that I had met in my whole lifetime. Earlier I told you that Natalie explained to me the story of one of the Dealer's top assassins. Well, the stage was now set for me to witness a job with the devil's man on earth; Lyle. He was an older black man with short white curly hair sprouting from every inch of his cheeks and neck. The top of his head was bare. He may have been short, but hell came in a small package. He turned to look me in the eyes.

"Kevin," he spoke in a deep growl. "We haven't met, but you are going to get to know me very well tonight. Do everything that I tell you, and you will sleep in your bed, safe and sound. Disobey me, and you will regret it."

I will never forget those eyes as long as I live. His eyes had to be the most wild and crazy eyes in existence. His pupils practically covered the whole eyeball. They shook with an intensity that I could not describe with words. His eyes looked not only at my eyes, but deep into my soul. His glare was more dangerous than any gun in the world. His stare fired bullets at me that paralyzed my vocal cords into only releasing a whimpering "Yes.".

"Good." He turned back to the steering wheel. He turned the key and ignited the engine to start. He pulled out of the forest, but continued to drive us further and further away from civilization. I do not know how long we drove, but at one point I wondered if it had been an hour since we had even seen a man-made structure. We eventually drove on a dirt road. After about a half hour we got to a clearing. Lyle parked the car about a hundred feet from the bank, where a lake met a stone covered beach. Instead of sand, the ground was covered in gray stones. For miles in every direction were only trees. Parked on the beach as well, was a large white van with tinted windows.

"Out," Lyle spoke. Natalie and I stepped out of the car. Lyle walked in the direction of the white van with Natalie and me close behind him. A man was sitting on the roof of the van waiting for us. The man was white with long brown wavy hair that fell to his shoulders. He was wearing a black jacket. His brown beard and mustache surrounded his grinning smile.

"Lyle! Good to see you my friend!" He exclaimed. When he spoke, mist erupted from his mouth. That was when I realized it was so cold we could see our breath. I had been so scared of Lyle that I did not even notice the temperature. The man hopped off of the van and shook Lyle's hand. "My friend we are going to blow your socks off tonight."

"I hope so," Lyle greeted. "It's good to see you Ivan." So the man's name was Ivan.

"Oh, I am excited tonight my friend. You and I will both be very happy by the end of this exchange," Ivan explained. He spoke with an accent that I did not recognize.

"Good. You have what I want?" Lyle asked. Ivan's smile grew.

"You bet I do," Ivan walked to the van and removed an already lit cigar from the roof. He placed it in his mouth. "Check this out." He punched the side of the van three times. The back doors swung open, and a woman was thrown out of it. She had a bag over her head, so I could not see her face. She was trying to scream, but something was muffling her voice. I could see that her wrists were zip tied together, as were her ankles. A large muscular bald man jumped out of the van with her, but I could tell that he was working with Ivan. "Friends, I would like to introduce you to my little brother Sergio."

Calling Sergio his "little" brother was a bit of a stretch, seeing that Sergio's muscles trumped Ivan's frail exterior.

"Is this the girl?" Lyle asked.

"I'll show you," Ivan smiled. "Sergio, would you be so kind?"

"Of course," Sergio spoke with the same accent as Ivan, but I still could not tell what accent it was. Sergio removed the bag from the woman's head, and I saw who she was. To my surprise, I knew her.

It was Arabella, the curvy woman who interviewed me before I started working for the Dealer. Her hair matched the color of the night sky. When I had first met her, she was a gorgeous woman beaming with confidence and superiority. Now, she looked like a nervous wreck with a towel shoved in her mouth. She looked behind her to see Sergio and Ivan. Then, she turned to us. I'll never forget how her demeanor completely changed when her eyes fell on Lyle. Her eyes widened, and her muffled screaming silenced. Her thrashing to escape had ceased. She just stared up at the man standing before her. The five of us had surrounded her in a circle. Lyle paced back and forth before her. Her eyes never left his direction. She was so fixated on Lyle that even the muscle bound Sergio was irrelevant in her mind. She knew things about Lyle that I didn't. It was written all over her face. I knew it, and just the idea of it made me shake. Somehow, this short old man scared her more than the two men who had just kidnapped her. Lyle stopped moving and scowled down at Arabella. He placed one hand on his hip.

"What's wrong? Did you not want to see me here tonight?" Lyle asked. "Well here I am so you're going to have to deal with it."

He stopped talking and just took the moment to stare her down. His gaze into my eyes had only lasted a moment, and it shook me to the core. I could only imagine what Arabella was feeling with this extended stare down. Her gaze never left his face.

"Funny story that I'm sure you've heard by now; we had three groups go out to sell yesterday. That is six people in total. All of them were attacked. Of those six people, four wound up dead. These two are the only ones that made it out." Lyle's arm slowly extended to point at Natalie and me. "The Dealer gave this girl the name Natalie. As of last week, she had never killed anyone. But last night, she had to kill someone for the first time in her life." His arm slowly dropped to his side. "Four good people were killed last night, Patrick, Ashley, Ryan, and Ned."

The only name that I recognized was Ned. Ned was the man who sold me cocaine that night. Now, he was dead.

"You wouldn't happen to know anything about that though right?" Lyle asked. Arabella frantically shook her head back and forth. Lyle's glare did not falter. "You see, that was a trick question, because I know that you know about this. I know that you've known that this attack was going to happen for some time. You want to hear how I know? Well, The Dealer has you plan some sales. Then he has others who organize these sales. But the thing is, you organized two of the three sales where the attacks took place last night. A striking similarity between those two attacks is that they were both conducted by the same gang. They're an unorganized and sloppy gang, but still a gang. Now they would have no knowledge that this sale was going to happen unless Natalie, Kevin, the Dealer, the buyer, or you told them. Natalie, Kevin, and the buyer would not have done that because that put their lives in danger. The Dealer didn't do it because he hates other gangs. So that leaves you. You gave extensive knowledge to them about where, when, and how the two sales were going to take place, didn't you?" Lyle tore the towel out of Arabella's mouth.

"I swear I didn't do any of that! I would never tell anyone any of that information! I promise!" Arabella screamed.

Lyle kneeled right in front of Arabella.

"The only thing that I hate more than liars, are people who think that they are smarter than me. You are both of those things," Lyle stood up. He popped open his holster, and placed his hand on the pistol. "Are you going to admit to these actions?" Arabella's face was bright red and tears were streaming down her face. Snot was dripping out of her nose. Her breathing was loud and heavy. Lyle removed the gun from the holster and pressed it against Arabella's forehead. Ivan, Sergio, and Natalie all drew their guns from their holsters as well and pointed them at Arabella. Seeing them do this, I followed along and did the same. "Last chance."

"Okay I did it!" Arabella screamed. Lyle moved his hand up to his ear.

"Excuse me for my hearing problems. What was that again?" Lyle asked.

"I did it."

"Louder!"

"I did it! I gave all of that information to the other gang and put six people's lives in danger!" Arabella admitted.

"Good." Lyle pulled his gun away from Arabella's forehead. She let out a sigh of relief. He paced in a circle around Arabella. He walked behind her, then to the space in front of her. The whole time Arabella did not move. When his back was to Arabella, he spoke again. "What did they do to get this information out of you?"

"What?" She asked, looking up at his back.

"They must have offered something to you before you gave them highly classified information on our sales. How did they convince you to become a narc?" Lyle asked.

Arabella's lip quivered.

"They threatened my life. They threatened the life of my mom," she choked out. She exhaled loudly. "They told me that they'd give me money."

"How much?" Lyle asked.

"It was sixty thousand dollars, or death," Arabella sobbed. Lyle sighed.

"So your life and sixty thousand dollars are worth more than four innocent lives?" Lyle asked, still with his back to Arabella. "Yes or no." Arabella choked up and heaved loudly.

"Y-yes," she cried.

"I appreciate the honesty, but I do have one more

question for you."

"What is it?" Arabella asked.

"Who else sold out information?" Lyle asked.

"No one!"

"I told you, stop lying to me," Lyle demanded. He turned to face her. He brought his face inches from hers. "You see, I know that you're lying because you only knew about two of the three sales. So you couldn't possibly have been able to sell out the third one. So who else gave out information?" I saw on Arabella's face that she realized that she had been completely defeated.

"The police officers who work for the Dealer," she explained.

"Oh come on. There are so many. You know that doesn't even narrow things down for me," Lyle snapped.

"McFowley and Granger," Arabella admitted.

That was my first connection with McFowley and Granger.

"Good," Lyle exhaled. "How do you know their real names?"

"When the other gang kidnapped me, they took me out deep into the mountains. They also took McFowley and Granger there with me. I had never seen them before. They addressed me by my first name. So, I assumed that the names they used for the police officers were their real names too," Arabella answered.

"Interesting," Lyle sighed.

"Could you let me go now? Please?" Arabella begged. "I... I just want to see my mom."

Lyle stood up and walked in my direction.

"Ivan, Sergio, she's all yours," Lyle called.

Natalie and I still held up our guns. Ivan and Sergio both put theirs away. Ivan withdrew a switchblade. He walked over to Arabella and cut the zip ties loose. She flinched when they were cut.

"Now, what I want you to do for me is stand up, but do not move from that spot. Understand?" Ivan explained. Arabella nodded. She stood up, but did not take a step in any direction. "Good. Now Strip."

"What?" She exclaimed.

"Oh come on, you heard me. Strip," Ivan instructed. Arabella looked at Lyle.

"Do it," Lyle demanded. Arabella removed her hoodie, and revealed a t-shirt. She looked at Ivan. He smiled and nodded. Arabella grabbed the bottom of her shirt, and pulled it up above her head. She dropped it on top of her sweatshirt. Ivan nodded again. Arabella stuck her thumbs beneath her sweatpants, and dropped them to her ankles. She kicked them on top of her shirt. She stood there in her underwear.

"It's really cold out," she protested. Goosebumps covered her skin.

"Would you do anything to live?" Ivan asked.

More tears rolled down her cheek.

"Y-yes." she spoke.

"Then keep going," Ivan instructed.

Arabella began wheezing again. She removed what little clothes she had left and dropped them into the pile next to her. She covered her chest with her right arm and her crotch with her left. Her legs crossed.

"Alright. So far, so go." Ivan smiled. "Now, I am going to need you to stand with your feet shoulder width apart. Also, I need you to hold your arms extended to your sides. Try to keep them as straight as possible. Hold your arms so that they are at a ninety-degree angle with your head and body. Like this." Ivan positioned his body as he explained it to her. Trembling, and reluctantly, she followed his orders. She closed her eyes. Ivan smiled. He removed a tape measurer from his pocket. Sergio removed a pen, paper, and a clip board from the van. Ivan extended the tape measurer from the top of Arabella's head, down to her feet. "Five foot five inches." He then measured the distance between Arabella's shoulders. "One foot three inches."

Ivan then continued to measure basically every dimension on her body. He measured the distance of her knee to her ankle. He measured the length of each of her fingers. He measured the distance between every joint of her body. Each time, he told Sergio the measurement, and he wrote it down. Every few minutes he tapped the charred end of his cigar onto the ground. When Arabella wiped a tear from her face, Ivan instructed her not to move. I could not tell how long that process lasted, but it must have been at least a half hour. In all likelihood, it felt way longer to Arabella than it did to me. Eventually, Ivan stopped and stepped away from her.

"Alright my friend, you can relax. I'm done," Ivan assured. Arabella covered her crotch and chest again. Ivan put an arm around Lyle's shoulders. "My friend, you have presented me with a gold mine!" Ivan rubbed Lyle's shoulders in celebration. "How much for her?"

"She is all yours, free of charge," Lyle answered.

"What?" Arabella asked.

"Allow me to explain," Ivan smiled. "In Columbia, it is such a huge business to sell people, mostly women, for one night. You see you are going to work for me and my brother."

"I'm going to be a slave?" Arabella asked.

"Oh slave is such a strong word. I prefer to call it a pleasure worker. That is a much prettier word," Ivan responded.

"I will not go to Columbia to be a sex slave!" Arabella snapped.

"Hey, you said that you would do anything to stay alive, didn't you?" Ivan laughed. He walked over to her. He put his arm around her shoulders, making her recoil in discomfort. "I am going to make so much money off of you. Your dimensions are perfect. Every man in Columbia will be dying to spend the night with you. You'll practically be a queen! The queen of Columbia! Think of it that way and it seems like a good thing."

"Please, anything but that," Arabella begged.

"You said that you didn't want to die, and now you won't. You should be grateful! Think about it, you'll be the 'Queen of Columbia'! That has a nice ring to it, doesn't it?" Ivan cheered. He removed two zip ties from his pocket. He bent down and bound her ankles with the zip tie. Then, he stood up and faced her. "I'm going to need to bind your wrists again." Arabella shook her head, but Ivan scowled at her. "One way or another, this zip tie is going around your wrist. Now you could either help me, or be an obnoxious brat about it."

Arabella submitted, and raised her wrists together. Ivan bound them together. Then, Arabella crossed her arms over chest. Ivan bent over and picked up the pile of her clothes from the ground. He placed them in her hands. She grabbed them, and tried to cover herself with them. Ivan looked toward Lyle.

"Hey Lyle, are we done here?" Ivan asked.

"I finished everything that I needed to do here," Lyle answered without even glancing at Arabella.

"You got any last words you wanna speak to the queen over here?" Ivan asked.

Lyle paused for a moment. "No," he answered.

Ivan looked at Arabella.

"Alright, back in the van you go, or chariot if you prefer to call it. That sounds more suitable for royalty," Ivan grabbed Arabella's arm and began dragging her to the van. She struggled and resisted. Then, she yelled to Lyle.

"You are a bad, bad man Lyle, and so many people are going to be happy when you die!" She yelled.

"Stop," Lyle called to Ivan. Ivan stopped walking. "I've had a change of heart. There is one last thing that I have to say to her majesty." Lyle turned to Arabella and walked right up to her. He pointed his finger in her face.

"I've got news for you lady. You brought this all upon yourself. You deserve everything that is coming to you. You betrayed the Dealer and that is why this is happening. This is not my doing. This is not anyone else's doing but your own. You are not smarter than any of us. No matter where you are in life, the Dealer will have one eye on you. Even when you think that you are alone, even when you think that no one is watching, someone is. You will never have any sense of privacy for as long as you live. The lives of four people now stand on your shoulders, and you will be painfully reminded of that every time that some dirty Colombian has his way with you. Every time that happens I want you to remember that you lost." Lyle stammered.

Sergio picked up Arabella and placed her in the car. He shut the door and she was gone. Ivan stood next to Lyle.

"Did you really need to say 'dirty Colombian'?" Ivan asked. Lyle just glared at him. Ivan raised his hands in surrender. "Okay, alright, it's your business. But seriously man, we should do business again sometime soon. I'm going to be making so much money off of this one. You sure you don't want any money?"

"Consider it a gift," Lyle responded.

"Merry fucking Christmas to us!" Sergio cheered. Ivan laughed at his joke.

Lyle turned to Natalie and me.

"You can put your guns away now," Lyle instructed. So we did. If there was anyone that I did not want to piss off in that moment, it was Lyle.

"Good work tonight guys. I'm so glad that we got to do business together," Ivan smiled. He removed the cigar from his mouth and blew out a cloud of smoke. His eyes lit up. "Oh Lyle, I nearly forgot!" He ran to his van and opened the driver's side door. He removed a package from it, and ran back to Lyle. He extended it out. "My friend, I almost forgot to give you these."

"What is it?" Lyle asked.

"Cigars straight from home," Ivan answered. "Just as a way to say 'thank you'."

"It's appreciated," Lyle answered.

Ivan began clapping. "It's always good to make new friends. Good night everyone. It was a pleasure doing business with you all. If you ever want to get rid of another person, I'm your guy," Ivan laughed. He and Sergio jumped into the van, and drove off. Lyle stood in the night air for a moment without speaking. He slowly exhaled, and a puff of the frigid mist came out of his mouth. He stared up at the moon. Natalie and I kept our mouths shut. His brown overcoat flapped in the wind. Then, slowly, he turned around. He stepped toward the two of us. He continued to walk toward the car. When our backs were to him, he spoke.

"Let's go," he said. Like the betas in a wolf pack, we followed quickly behind him without question. Natalie sat in the front passenger seat. And I was in the back just like we sat on the way there. The car ride back was even scarier than the ride there if you could believe that. The terrifying thing about the car ride there was the fear of not knowing what was going to happen. What made the ride back so scary was knowing just who Lyle was. That interaction with Lyle raised more questions than answers. I had no idea how many times he did something such as that. He was obviously very close with the Dealer. I imagined Lyle as the Dealer's right hand man. I couldn't imagine anyone closer to the Dealer than he was. What scared me about Lyle was just how cold and dead pan his delivery was. He never cursed, screamed, or lost himself in his emotions. It all seemed so routine for him.

Finally, we made our way back to the clearing with our other car. Lyle parked the car and looked at us.

"Arabella got what she deserved," he spoke. "She put your lives in danger. She almost got you killed. I want you two to remember that. I didn't do anything unnecessary tonight. I did what had to be done. She put your lives at risk and that will not be tolerated." He reached over to the glove compartment and removed two large orange envelopes. The envelope had to have been taller than my head. He handed one to Natalie, and one to me. "This is your reward for a job well done tonight. Kevin, Monday at six in the morning I need you to be outside of Stewart's Tavern for another job. Other than that, the two of you should enjoy your weekends without working. You've earned it. You may go now."

So we took our envelopes and left. We got back into our original car. I sat in the passenger seat, and Natalie sat in the driver's seat. She turned the car on, and pulled out of the forest and back onto the road. I saw that the time read three thirty seven in the morning. I awkwardly peered at Natalie.

"I'm really sorry," I apologized.

"For what?" Natalie asked.

"I had no idea that you never killed anyone before. You just took action and shot that guy without any hesitation. I choked up and couldn't rise to the occasion. You just took action. You did it so well that I thought that you had done it before. I'm so sorry that you had to do that," I explained.

"Saying that I never killed anyone before this week is kind of stretching the truth, but I just couldn't stand the thought of never seeing you again," Natalie answered. A single tear rolled down her face.

"You did not kill Brian. It was a freak accident and it will never happen again," I spoke.

"You can say that all that you want. My mom did. It won't affect how I see it," Natalie answered. "I would kill that man a million times again if it meant seeing you. I mean that. I killed him and I don't regret it. He would've killed you if I didn't act."

"Thank you Natalie. I really mean that. I am really glad that you're here for me. I think that this world would have driven me crazy by now if I hadn't met you," I said. Another tear rolled down her cheek. "Oh don't start crying."

"I'm not crying," she said wiping her face. "I feel the same way. If I didn't have you then I would have gone crazy by now. I couldn't think of anyone else in the world that I would rather spend this much time with." Her saying that made me smile like a big dork.

"Sometimes I wonder if I'm a piece of shit," I groaned, leaning my head back on the car seat.

"Well I know that you're a piece of shit," Natalie joked. I smirked at her joke, even though I wasn't in a laughing mood. "But in all seriousness, that's okay. Sometimes I wonder if I'm a piece of shit too." We then sat in silence for a moment. Natalie placed a hand on my knee. "Look at the bright side. The worst is over. Soon we can go to work feeling safe again."

"Apparently Lyle wants to do a job with just me on Monday. I don't know how that's going to go," I responded.

"Well it certainly can't go any worse than today went," Natalie said.

"I sure do hope not."

The entire ride home we talked. Our conversations led to so many different topics. We didn't even talk about work after a while. It was so incredible how well Natalie and I got along. I feel like I've never been able to get along with anyone as well as I have with Natalie. By the end of the car ride, we were relaxed enough to have conversations that made us laugh, sometimes even gut busting laughter. I was so tired, but speaking with Natalie was so intriguing that sleep had completely left my mind. At around five in the morning, we realized that it had been over ten hours since either of us had eaten anything. So, we stopped at a gas station for food. She was looking at all of the candy and bags of chips.

"Natalie, you don't know how to live," I said, putting a hand on her shoulder. "Observe."

"Okay I guess," Natalie agreed. I then proceeded to buy a five-dollar box of gas station pizza. We brought it into the car and opened the box. "This literally looks awful." She giggled.

"I know that it looks bad, but you can trust me, this is the greatest food in the whole world," We both took a bite of the slice in our hands. She started laughing.

"Oh my God, this is so bad," she laughed. We both just looked at each other while our laughs synced up.

"No, it tastes good," I argued. She dabbed her finger into the pizza sauce, and slapped it onto my cheek. "Oh you son of a bitch!"

By that time, it seemed more like a big sleepover rather than collusion. But by the time I got dropped off at Stewart's Tavern, I already missed her. I got into my car which was parked in the Stewart's Tavern parking lot, and drove home to my apartment. At around six in the morning, I was home. I plopped myself onto my bed with the orange envelope in my hand. Inside of it was money. I had to have counted it about a dozen times over because I couldn't believe what I was looking at.

Twenty-five thousand dollars.

I was scared to fall asleep. I was afraid of what I would dream of. I was afraid that I would close my eyes and see Lyle. I was afraid of closing my eyes and seeing a piece of skull flip through the air. I was afraid to see Arabella naked and afraid. I was afraid to see Ivan and Sergio again. Thankfully for me, none of that happened. What I did dream about did surprise me though.

I dreamed of Natalie.

Chapter 13

"I know that I should have hated Arabella, I really do. But I couldn't help but feel bad for her in a way. She put Natalie's life in danger, mine too, and I hate her for that. On the other hand, her whole life was up rooted. It was like seeing a bee sting you. You're hurt, but the bee is in a whole lot more pain than you are," Jonan explained.

With a quivering hand, Samuel removed the glasses from his face. He looked up to Jonan with a solemn look.

"I'm going to need you to be very clear with your answers to the following questions, and I need you to be absolutely positive when you answer me. Do you understand boy?" Samuel asked. Jonan nodded silently, staring at his hands. "So this girl was taken from the United States and forced into the sex trade?" Jonan nodded. "This man Lyle, to your understanding, is a hitman?" Jonan nodded. "Finally, this is my most important question. Are you suggesting that Granger and McFowley were involved with the illegal drug trade?"

"You have to belie-"

"You listen to me and you listen well!" Samuel snapped,

slamming his hand on the table. "There are a whole lot of people in this building who claim that Granger and McFowley were good men, and would take it as an insult if you told them that they were criminals! I did not know either of them personally, but it is not in your best interest to say these things if they are not true!"

"It is true! Officer, I'm a dead man walking! I have nothing to lose! What good would it bring me if I lied about this?" Jonan pleaded. "They pissed off the Dealer and that's why they're dead!"

"How do you expect me to go out there and tell Granger and McFowley's friends that they are criminals?" Samuel asked.

"But listen man, you gotta be extra careful who you tell this information to. I swear you need to be absolutely positive that they are trustworthy," Jonan warned.

"And why the hell is that?" Samuel asked.

"Because the Dealer has other police officers that work for him," Jonan whispered. His next sentence was so quiet that he was practically mouthing the words. "There are probably more in this building, working on this case, listening to our conversation, and I bet that you even know one of them."

Samuel said nothing for a moment. He just sat there at the table, staring at Jonan and contemplating what he had just said. He was scratching the scar on the side of his face.

"How do you know that I am not working for the Dealer?" Samuel whispered. Jonan started chuckling quietly. "What's so funny?"

Jonan leaned forward. His eyes widened and he smiled like a crazy person. "I don't," Jonan sat back, laughing.

Samuel stood up and walked out of the room. He closed the door behind him. Samuel walked throughout the hallways until he made his way to Frank's office. Samuel knocked on the door as he let himself in.

"Oh Sam, I got you a gift," Frank tossed a cassette tape to Samuel. He caught it in one of his hands. "That is a recording of the voicemail found on Casey's phone. You can listen to that when you get the chance. You're welcome."

"Thank you," Samuel answered, putting it in his pocket. "Can I speak to you about some sensitive information?"

"Sam, if this is about the baby making, there is a pill for that," Frank smiled. He saw that Samuel was being serious. "You need to lighten up sometimes. Sure talk to me about anything."

Samuel closed the door to Frank's office. "Okay, you are going to think that I sound crazy," Samuel huffed.

"Just say it man. I promise you that I won't think that you're crazy," Frank assured.

"Now when I say that this is sensitive information, I really do mean it. You can't tell this to anyone that you do not one hundred percent trust. You really need to understand that," Samuel explained.

"Look, I promise you that I won't overreact, and I won't tell anyone without consulting you first," Frank assured.

"The boy is telling me that Granger and McFowley were involved in the drug trade," Samuel admitted.

"That boy had better hope that the judge sentences him to life, because if I get my hands on him, then I'm killing him. I'm telling the chief!" Frank shrieked.

"What happened to not overreacting?" Samuel asked.

"How do you expect me to just take that information and sit on it?" Frank asked. "Also, there are cameras in that room with people watching and listening. They have to know. You should know that Sam."

"I do know that. I am just afraid of how the other officers will react to this," Samuel stated.

"Well, obviously this kid is crazy," Frank stated. Samuel did not respond. Frank turned his head in frustration. "You-You don't believe him do you?" Samuel did not reply. Frank's eyebrows bent in frustration. "Sam!"

"He was so convincing! He showed real raw emotion when telling his stories. He genuinely was feeling those emotions when telling me his stories. It was way too real to be a lie," Samuel pressed.

"And he can thank the academy when they give him his Oscar," Frank snapped.

"You can't tell me that he is lying without disproving it," Samuel continued.

"He's lying. There I did it," Frank replied.

"So everything that he says is instantly discredited because of a crime that he hasn't even been convicted of yet?" Samuel asked.

"How can you even think that he didn't do it?" Frank

asked.

"What happened to innocent until proven guilty? You even said that they don't think the gun had been fired in weeks."

"We are looking for a second gun! Once we find it, this kid's ass is ours," Frank rebutted.

"Well then, until you find this mystery gun, you need to treat this kid as if he's innocent. Therefore, his word is good as any other citizen's word," Samuel pressed.

Frank slammed his fist on the desk. "Fine. But what do you want me to do? Look inside McFowley and Granger's house for cocaine? How do you expect me to get a warrant for this?" Frank asked.

"You don't need one," Samuel replied.

"What are you on about?" Frank asked.

"McFowley has a wife. If you have consent to inspect their house, then you don't need a warrant," Samuel explained.

"Yes, hello miss. Your dead husband's alleged killer says that he might be a drug dealer. May I look in your home for cocaine?" Frank mocked.

"Sugar coat it to the point that you'd get diabetes from the sentence," Samuel advised. "And don't bring a drug dog to McFowley's house. Then she would know that something is up."

"Sugar coating. Got it," Frank answered. "What about Granger's place? He lived alone right?"

"Yeah I think he did," Samuel answered.

"So we can search there too, right?" Frank asked.

"Yes we can. If McFowley's Wife doesn't let us in, then we have a problem," Samuel stated.

Frank got up and put his coat on. "I agree. Let's go," Frank suggested.

"I can't," Samuel answered.

"Why not?" Frank asked.

"Jonan is still telling me his story," Samuel answered.

"Jesus that kid can talk," Frank sighed.

"You don't think that I know that yet?" Samuel asked sarcastically. "Now remember, sugar coating."

"Yeah yeah yeah, sugar coating," Frank answered.

An hour later, Frank arrived on the porch of McFowley's house. He ran his fingers through his hair anxiously. He exhaled strongly, raising his hand to the door as if to knock on it, but then nervously pulled away. He whispered to himself; "Sugar coat. Sugar coat,". Then, Frank knocked on the door. An attractive pale brunette woman opened the door. Her cheeks were red, and there were balled up tissues in her hands.

"Hello?" She greeted.

"Good evening. Are you Mrs. McFowley?" Frank asked.

"Yes that would be me. Who are you?" She asked.

Frank revealed his badge. "Officer Frank Stanley. I was

a co-worker of your husband. On behalf of all of us down at the station, I am sorry for your loss. I can't even fathom what you are going through," Frank began.

"Oh thank you. That means a lot to me," Mrs. McFowley answered.

"How are you holding up?" Frank asked.

"Well, I'm still trying to understand everything," she answered.

"If it makes you feel any better, we are still trying to understand everything too. Now, I have a request for you. I think that if I were to take look around the house, it might help us put the man who did this behind bars quicker. Would you give consent for that?" Frank asked.

"Oh, of course. I would do anything to help. Come on in," she invited. Frank stepped inside the house. He looked around at the white kitchen. Then, Frank saw one of the kids sleeping on the couch.

"Please try to be quiet. I just managed to get him to fall asleep. He was up all night," Mrs. McFowley requested.

"Of course," Frank whispered. "Now, is there any place in particular where Andrew spent most of his time? I think that would be a good place to start."

"Well, Andrew would spend time in the living room watching T.V, in our bedroom of course, and he also spent a lot of time in the garage. There is an old car in there that his father owned. The car is a piece of crap but Andrew spent hours upon hours working on it. Me and the kids never really went in there, so that was really Andrew's space," Mrs. McFowley answered.

"Thank you. I think that I'll start with the garage," Frank whispered. Mrs. McFowley lead him to the garage. Since the wife and kids do not go into the garage, it would be the perfect place to hide illegal items. Frank stepped in and closed the door behind him. Flipping on the light switch, he saw all of the junk displaced in the room. There was the old car, just like Mrs. McFowley said there was. All around the car were tool boxes, and tools scattered about the room. Frank checked the toolboxes and found nothing of value. He checked the buckets and only found more tools. He checked inside of the gasoline jugs only to find gasoline. He checked inside the refrigerator, but only saw beer cans and other food items. He did not see anything out of the ordinary. Then, He turned to the tool desk. There was exactly what you would expect, more tools. Again, there was nothing out of the ordinary. Then, Frank turned to the car.

He opened the car door and inspected the inside. The car was an actual heap of trash. It was rusted everywhere, only had half a steering wheel, the seat belts were chewed by rats, the gas pedal was missing, it had no engine, only three wheels, and the interior's smell made Frank's nose recoiled. It smelled like old leather was mixed with gasoline and rat feces. He checked the glove compartment to see nothing but a box of cigarettes. Frank checked inside to find a single unused cigarette. Frank smiled as he removed it from the box and put it in his pocket. Frank looked inside all of the compartments and still found nothing.

He looked around the car for twenty minutes. He began thinking that he was in over his head. He was by himself, and did not even know what he was looking for. He was about ready to go back to the station. He thought he should just try to get a warrant, so that he could have a crew and a drug sniffing dog. That would make things so much easier. But then, something caught his eye... the back seat.

There was a noticeable bend at one of the corners where the back of a person's knees would rest if they were sitting in the car. Across the left corner was a much defined crease, and the leather that made up that corner was not fully attached to the seat. Frank ran his fingers along that corner. He lifted the flap of leather from the seat. He moved his head closer to the space between the seats which was now revealed by lifting the leather.

"Oh my God."

Chapter 14

"You don't think that I know that?" Samuel asked sarcastically. "Now remember, sugar coating."

"Yeah, yeah, yeah, sugar coating," Frank answered. Frank turned and left his office. Samuel left as well, but he went in the other direction. He went in the direction of the interrogation room. Samuel opened the door, and entered the room to see Jonan sitting alone handcuffed to the table, just as Samuel had left him. Samuel sat down.

"Would you care to continue?" Samuel asked.

"Alright. So remember how Lyle asked me to see him Monday morning?" Jonan asked.

"Yes," Samuel answered.

"Well, that was this past Monday. Today is Saturday, so that makes this five days ago."

I was absolutely terrified to see what Lyle wanted to do with me. I was afraid that he might even kill me. Spoiler alert, he didn't. So I was waiting outside of Stewart's Tavern just like I normally do at seven in the morning. The dinky little brown sedan pulled up to me. It looked like it had to be twenty years old or older. The window rolled down and Lyle was there wearing a fedora and sunglasses. He spoke out to me.

"Get in."

Just those two words. I got in the car like the obedient dog that I was. Then we were off. The drive began.

"So, um, how's it going man?" I asked. He just sat there driving. "I really appreciate all that money from the other day man. That was um, really cool of you to, um, you know, give me that kind of money. I've never seen that much money, let alone have it." I ran my fingers through my hair. "Tell the boss man that I appreciate the razor. I can grow a beard. I had one, you know, but um, I had to get rid of it because of, you know, the rules and stuff." Still, Lyle sat quietly. "Mason and Bill came and dropped the razor off at my place. They're really cool guys. Especially that Mason guy. Me and him are tight you know? I don't know if you know them though." I paused. "That Bill guy is really chill, you know I think that you and him would get along really well because you guys are similar. Similar, good similar, not like, bad similar. Like, I think you guys would have a good conversation together." Lyle remained quiet. "You get it? Like, because you're both quiet, and I said that you'd make great conversation? Like, as a joke. The joke is that-"

"Stop talking," Lyle spoke.

"Okay."

The rest of the car ride lasted hours. It was strange. I had been all over the place with Natalie that I had thought that I had seen every inch of the state. As it turns out, I was wrong. Lyle took me to places that I had never seen before.

They were all desolate roads. There were practically no other cars on the roads that he took me on. We drove for hours like that. Natalie and I typically stopped and switched with another car along the way. I assumed that we were going to do that too. As it turned out, I was wrong. We swapped cars so many times that I lost count. I don't know how many cars this guy owns, but it is clearly a crap ton. At 2:34 pm, I realized that we had been driving on a dirt road though some mountains for quite some time.

"Kevin," Lyle finally spoke. "I need you to do me a favor."

"Of course," I answered.

"I need you to follow my lead and stay quiet. I will be working out a deal. Only speak when spoken to. You understand?"

"Yes," I answered.

"Good," Lyle replied. "Now we will be pulling up to a house in these mountains. These people will ask us to surrender our weapons. You will have to give them anything that you brought with you. Did you bring your pistol?"

"Yes," I answered.

"Good" Lyle said. "Can you play dumb whenever they speak to you?"

"That comes naturally to me," I chuckled.

"Good," Lyle continued. "If I tell you to do something, I need you to do it."

"I will," I answered. Lyle removed his sunglasses and looked at me with his piercing eyes.

"I need you to not screw up. If you screw up, we could both end up dead," He warned.

I gulped hard. "I understand."

The car pulled up to a large gate blocking the road. My heart began racing. Two men with what appeared to be assault rifles approached the car. One of them tapped the window next to Lyle. Lyle rolled down the window and stayed solid as a rock.

"The name is Lyle. I am here to speak with Sir James Tulken," Lyle told them. The man nodded to the other one, who hit a button on the side of the gate that allowed it to open up. Lyle rolled the window up and continued driving. Lyle looked at me. "You need to remain calm." I nodded.

The car parked in front of a giant mansion. When I say that this mansion was giant, I mean it was the biggest house that I had ever laid my eyes on. It was no taller than the trees, but it still appeared at least ten times the size of my apartment. It was at least twice the size of a typical two story suburban household. Lyle parked near the front door. Lyle reached between my knees and opened the glove compartment. He removed a shoebox, and then closed the glove compartment. Three large muscular white men wearing over coats stepped up to our car.

"Get out," Lyle instructed. So I did.

"You're Lyle?" One of the men asked.

"That would be me," Lyle's face turned into one of kindness and friendliness, which was the last thing that I expected to see from that monster. "Mr. Tulken is available for us to speak correct?"

"Yes he is, I am sorry for asking this, but it's just a precaution," the man began. "Do you guys have any weapons on you?"

"Oh, of course that isn't too much to ask," Lyle replied. Seeing him smile was one of the creepiest things I had ever seen. Lyle withdrew a handgun from a holster on his side and handed it to the man. "It's all yours."

"Thank you for understanding." The man took it from Lyle's hand. "What about the kid?"

"Boy, will you please hand him your pistol?" Lyle requested. I did as he asked, and handed the man my pistol.

"I need to ask again before you can see Mr. Tulken. Can we pat you down?" The man asked Lyle. Lyle extended his arms.

"Pat away," he invited. The two other men, who had not spoken a word, patted us both down. After it was done, then man spoke again.

"Alright you boys can come on in," he invited. We entered and followed the three men. We walked past other rooms and I saw how these people lived. In one room was two men getting a lap dance from strippers. In another room I saw two men doing lines of cocaine. In another room, three German shepherds were tearing a human sized doll limb from limb. There was one consistency with every single room. They all had cocaine spilled somewhere in the room, whether it was the corner, or on a table, or the center of the room, all of them had a spill of cocaine somewhere.

But then, we made it to a room that appeared to be a library. In that room were five giant men. They were all standing in a circle around the center of the room. All of the men had a German Shepard on a leash. In the center of the room was a table with four chairs. On one side of the table were two men. One man was a scrawny man in a suit, and the other was a semi muscular man with long red wavy hair. He was wearing a black tank top and jeans. He turned to look at us, and smiled a devilish grin that I had only seen before in movies with Jack Nicholson.

"I can't tell you just how happy I am to see you guys!" He growled.

"Good evening Mr. James Tulken," Lyle extended a hand to shake his hand. Tulken returned the handshake.

"Please sit down. You're mister, um-"

"You can just call me Lyle."

"I like that name. It's easy to remember, not made up like some of these crazy, ghetto ass, foreign names." James Tulken smiled.

"I brought gifts," Lyle said gleefully. He opened up the shoe box and removed a container of ten cigars.

"Oh look at these babies!" Tulken smiled a toothy smile.

"I got these from a business associate of mine," Lyle said, as he opened up the container.

"Where are these from? Cuba?" Tulken asked.

"Columbia," Lyle answered, lighting a cigar and handing it to Tulken. Tulken leaned back and took a puff on the cigar, and exhaled with a satisfied moan.

"God damn that is fine," Tulken exclaimed, extending his arms into the air chuckling. Every one of Tulken's mannerisms reminded me of a wolf. His voice reminded me of a wolf's growl. His smile reminded me of the way a wolf would bare it's teeth right before they killing its prey. His pointed nose reminded me of a wolf's snout, smelling for something to sink its teeth into. His hair cascaded like a wolf's fur.

"I am glad that you are enjoying it," Lyle smiled.

"You got any more gifts for me?" Tulken laughed. He inhaled on his cigar again.

"Actually, yes," Lyle answered. Tulken looked at Lyle in surprise.

"Alright! Keep em coming baby! Yeah!" Tulken yelled. Lyle reached into the shoe box and withdrew a tiny plastic baggy filled with cocaine. It was the same size as the bag that I bought from Ned. Lyle placed it on the table. Tulken saw it, and put his cigar on the table to inspect the baggy. His smile disappeared as he looked intensely into the bag.

"Well hello there my little friend," Tulken smiled. He looked at me. "Hey spick, what is your deal? Tu hablo englase?" He asked, tapping my shoulder.

"Todas las fabricaciones de vida creadas por nuestra mente sólo son un enigma," I said.
"Hahaha me too!" He laughed, smacking my shoulder. Tulken removed a knife, and stabbed it into the table. He dragged it across to cut open the plastic bag, clearly not caring about the large gash that he just put into the table. He dipped the tip of the knife into the bag to take some of the small amount of cocaine on the tip. He lifted it into the air

near me. "You first."

My heart bounced out of my chest. He wanted me to snort cocaine? Why? Why me? I was afraid of what it would do to me. I had done cocaine once before, but that time was at a bar where everyone was under the influence of some kind of substance. This was terrifying. I looked to Lyle, who nodded at me. He wanted me to go along with it. So I gulped, leaned my head forward, and sniffed the cocaine into my nose.

I instantly felt a sharp burning sensation in my nostril. It stung like a thousand hornets had been released into my nose. I held my hands up to my nose and jerked my head back. I outwardly gasped and began moaning. This was stronger than the cocaine that I had done with Ned, way stronger. My nose felt like it was on fire. My eyes were tearing up. It was like eating every piece of spicy food in the world at once. I was clearly in physical pain.

"Haha!" Tulken exclaimed. "Yeah Spick! Great job man! Yeah!" That was when he held the rest of the bag to his nose and took a sniff. He pulled back in reaction to the drug. "Woo hoo! God damn Lyle! This feels like you just lit off Fourth of July fireworks in my nose!"

"So you like it?" Lyle smiled.

"Like it? I think that I love this more than my girlfriends. You got any more of this stuff?" Tulken asked.

"I actually brought you a kilogram, completely free, as a gift," Lyle removed a large package from the shoebox. My jaw dropped. A kilogram? For free? That had to be at least a hundred thousand dollars. Why was he just giving all of that away?

"You, you what?" Tulken asked. He was clearly just as shocked as I was. Tulken reached for the package, and Lyle quickly pulled it away.

"Not quite yet. I want us to make an agreement first. Then when our meeting is done, you can get your gift," Lyle said.

Tulken began chuckling. "Oh my friend you are a tease," Tulken laughed. He clapped his hands together. "Alright. Let's get down to business so that we can get to play time faster. Now your stuff is good, I mean really good. I have never had cocaine light up my nostrils like that before in my life. So how about we do this, you get me five kilograms of this stuff a week, and I will give you half a million each week for that." That was when the man in the suit sitting next to Tulken spoke up.

"Uh, sir, I am sorry to interrupt you, but half a million is too much for five kilograms. At least bring the price down to four hundred thousand," the man said.

"It's my money Berkovich, I can do what I want with it," Tulken replied. Berkovich's knees closed together.

"Well, sir, I don't think that the return on investment would be satisfactory to you if you made that deal," Berkovich argued sheepishly. Tulken looked back to Lyle.

"I'm sorry Lyle. I'll give you four hundred fifty thousand a week for five kilograms. How does that sound to you?" Tulken asked.

"I'm sorry to interrupt again sir, but even four hundred fifty thousand for five kilograms wouldn't be satisfactory," Berkovich said. Tulken looked disappointed.

"Berkovich, I am trying to have an adult conversation between myself and Lyle," Tulken snapped. He picked up the tiny bag of cocaine and snorted whatever was left in it. Then, he recoiled from the sensation. He grunted as he punched the side of his own head multiple times. "Woo! Berkovich this is some five hundred-thousand-dollar shit right here! If you tried it, then you would understand that this stuff would be selling like hot cakes!" His voice changed to something more vicious and sinister. The cocaine was changing him. I could see it. I was feeling what I had sniffed too. My heart was racing and my forehead was sweating bullets. Staying in that chair took all of my willpower.

"No thank you sir. Cocaine isn't my forte'," Berkovich declined. Tulken chuckled. He took his knife and stabbed it into the table so that it was standing upright. He chuckled as it made a loud clank. Me and Berkovich flinched, while Lyle remained rock solid.

"Sorry about him. You know how bothersome financial consultants could be at times, right?" Tulken said to Lyle, laughing an evil laugh.

"Oh don't mind them. They are just people who try to tell you how to use your own money," Lyle chuckled. Tulken went into an episode of hysterical laughter. His face went turned bright crimson, and his mouth snared.

"God dammit, you are funny aren't you!" Tulken screamed. He slammed his hand on the table multiple times. He slammed his hand so hard that blood busted out of the knuckle. He didn't even acknowledge his injury. This man was psychotic. "So how do you feel about the half a million every single week?"

"I would say that-" Lyle began.

"Hey!" Tulken yelled to one of his guards. "Put on Slowhand." The guard walked to one of the tables that had a radio on it. He pressed the play button, and Eric Clapton's song "Cocaine" began playing. "Sorry to interrupt you. My absolute favorite song is this one. What about you?"

"Ah yes, great song. It suits you," Lyle chuckled.

Tulken again released a very loud boisterous laugh. "Oh, you are a riot Lyle! I swear!" Tulken yelled. His face was red as a brick.

"I was going to say that half a million would be justified. But what if we did six kilograms for six hundred fifty thousand a week?" Lyle asked.

Berkovich looked shocked. "Mr. Tulken, that deal is not going to-" he began.

"Gentlemen," Tulken called to the guards. "Would two of you please escort Mr. Berkovich to the basement? Please?"

Berkovich looked terrified. "Sir! Please! This is unnecessary!" He begged. Two of the guards silently lifted Berkovich from his chair. They carried him out of the room. He grabbed the doorway. "Sir, please! Tell them to put me down! This is unnecessary! Please let me go!"

"Shut up!" Tulken screamed as he chucked his knife in Berkovich's direction. The knife stabbed into the wall right next to Berkovich's head. "I told you to keep your God damn mouth shut, and you kept running your mouth! Now take your fucking attitude, and fuck off!" The men pried Berkovich's hands from the door and swept him away. I was sure that whatever was about to happen to Berkovich would not be good. Tulken turned to us and sat back down. "I would like to deeply apologize for that man. I would like to agree to the deal that you offered. Can you get me six kilograms a week?"

"I can do that," Lyle confirmed. Tulken smiled.

"Excellent," Tulkin growled. He leaned forward. "I look forward to working together for a long, long time."

The conversation dragged on for a while, but it ended with Lyle handing Tulken the gift of a kilogram of cocaine. We were escorted back to our car. I remained quiet as we drove. We drove down the mountain, through all of those winding roads, and eventually back to a car to switch into. When we switched into that car and began driving off, Lyle looked at me and began speaking.

"James Earl Tulken was the kingpin of the gang that attempted to kill you," Lyle admitted. "I took you there because I needed to have someone with me. That was an important task for us."

"So what now? We are working with the enemy?" I asked.

"Of course not. I'd rather die than work with that human waste of flesh," Lyle answered.

I was confused. "So what were we there for? Why did you give him a free kilogram of cocaine? What was the point?" I asked.

"I actually gave him nine hundred fifty milligrams of cocaine," Lyle corrected.

"Okay how does fifty milligrams make a difference?" I asked.

"The cocaine that was in the tiny bag was normal cocaine. The Dealer worked extra hard on it to make sure that it was A+ level cocaine. That way it would entice an addict such as James Earl Tulken. But that kilogram package only has nine hundred and fifty milligrams of cocaine," Lyle continued.

"So what is the other fifty milligrams?" I asked.

"That is a secret ingredient," Lyle answered. "Ideally, if everything goes well, he'll be using that batch multiple times a day over the course of the next few days. Then, after a few days of exposure, he'll take in one more puff of the drug. But this time will be different. He'll whip his nose to make sure that he sniffed all of it. The problem is, when he does that, he'll find blood on his fingers. Not a little bit. There will be a hell of a lot of blood. That is when drug kingpin James Earl Tulken will disappear off the face of the planet. You will not have anything else to worry about, because the only man who wanted your head will be dead."

"But we can get caught for murder so easily, can't we?" I asked.

"You see Kevin, these crime movies will lead people to believe that there are ways to leave absolutely no evidence at a crime scene, but they are wrong. It is absolutely impossible to leave no evidence. So, I use that to my advantage. I do horrible things to people, but I only do those things to people who have also done horrible things. Let's say Arabella escaped and went to the police. She would then have to admit to them that she was an accomplice to wide scale drug trafficking. If these guys realize that we killed James Earl Tulken, then they would have to tell the police that they also ran a wide scale drug trafficking ring. Then they would all get thrown in jail. So no criminal in their right mind would admit to wrongdoing in order to help the police. That would involve putting them in trouble as well. Always know your enemy's weaknesses," Lyle explained. "I always say; if you believe that you are the smartest man in the room, then you have already lost. That man believed that he was smarter than us, and we just proved him wrong."

I struggled to understand what he was saying."But, but isn't what we just did a little over the line?" I asked.

"Sometimes we need to cross the line in order to make sure that it still exists," Lyle answered. "This mission was important, and I hope that you understand that."

"Alright. I guess that we did need to do that then." I slumped in my seat.

"Now, that brings me to my proposal," Lyle began. "How would you like to make more money than you could ever even imagine? You would only have to work once every two weeks, and you'd be making way more than you do now."

"What would it involve?" I asked.

"You would begin working with me and-"

"Hey, no way man! I am not doing that! Look Lyle, I respect you for what you do, you know, being able to do the things that you do. But I can't do that. It's just not the kind of person I am. I am sorry but no more kill missions! I want to keep selling with Natalie just like I've been doing for the past three months. I like it, and I am more than satisfied with the amount of money that I am making," I answered.

"Well, I respect your honesty," Lyle replied. "I will respect your wishes."

We did not speak for the remainder of the car ride until we got back to Stewart's Tavern. Lyle handed me a suitcase from the back seat of the car. He looked at me and said;

"This is your pay for the day. Congratulations. The Dealer will call you later this week when it is safe to resume work again." And just like that, Lyle was gone. But my meeting with Lyle was not the craziest part of my trip. The craziest part was counting the money that I earned that day. It was the most money I had ever received in my life...

Fifty thousand dollars.

Chapter 15

The following days were a constant nightmare. I stayed inside all day, every day. I was constantly peering through my blinds for anyone suspicious, or anyone that I would not want to see. I always saw Mason and Bill's car outside, so yes there was someone that I did not want to see. But I also constantly checked the locks on my windows. I kept a running tab on where various items were in the apartment, so that if I saw any suspicious movement, then I could react properly. I was constantly afraid that one of Tulken's men might break in to hurt me.

No matter how hard I tried, I couldn't get a few images out of my head. I couldn't stop thinking of Berkovich being dragged off to the basement. I have no idea what happened to him there, but it had to be bad. He was punished for basically nothing. Tulken was just a drug addict with an anger problem. I also couldn't get the idea of that shard of skull flipping through the air and landing on the ground. Those thoughts kept replaying in my head over and over again.

It wasn't until Thursday that something finally happened. It was a call from none other than the Dealer himself.

"Hello?" I answered the phone eagerly.

"Kevin, this is the Dealer," he greeted. "It has been a while since we last spoke."

"Um, yeah it has," I stuttered.

"Kevin, I need to congratulate you," The Dealer began.

"Me?" I asked confused.

"Yes, of course. Lyle told me that he was impressed by your performance over the past week," The Dealer explained. "You followed Lyle's instruction perfectly, and everything went according to plan."

"Um, how did everything go according to plan?" I gulped.

"James Earl Tulken is dead. He took his last breath late last night. He owned the only cocaine ring in this part of the country that rivaled our size. We now control all of Wisconsin, Michigan, Illinois and Indiana. That means that we are back in business. We can now start selling again without fear of another attack. Lyle said that he couldn't have pulled it off without you Kevin," The Dealer explained. My eyes widened. "I will be meeting with McFowley and Granger at the Pigeon Dock Friday night to discuss with them what to do about their betrayal."

"So, what does that mean for me?" I asked.

"It means that you are a much more valuable asset to me than I had initially predicted," The Dealer answered. "You have earned my respect, and trust. Those two things are very hard to earn from me, so congratulations."

"Um, thank you sir," I gulped. "So now what?"

"We continue selling," the Dealer answered. "We start again tomorrow. Natalie will pick you up tomorrow morning at seven like usual. Understood?"

"Yes, understood," I answered.

"Good." The Dealer hung up the phone.

I stood there in silence for a moment. Then, I started throwing my fists in the air, playing the air guitar and break dancing in excitement. I had just made it through a week long ordeal that made me fear for my life. The best part about it ending was that I would get to see Natalie again.

That day I made a purchase. I bought a speed boat. It was a dinky little thing that could fit a maximum of three people at once. Obviously I wasn't going to buy anything grand in fear of somebody being suspicious. The man that I handed the money to was confused about why the money that I handed him was freezing and stiff as a board, but I just told him that I misplaced it in an icebox. Yes, I would like to thank the academy.

The point is that I rented out a spot at a small dock on the coast of lake Michigan that wasn't too far from the Pigeon Dock where McFowley and Granger were going to meet the Dealer. I did that in case something were to happen that would require me to go far, far away. I had no idea what I was preparing for, but I knew that it would be a good idea to expect the unexpected.

That weekend I made more money than I ever even seen in my whole life. I had made seventy-five thousand dollars in a weekend. In my old job, I wouldn't have even made that in two years. The means that lead me to make that money was what scared me. I assisted in enslaving someone, and killing somebody else. It's not like they were innocent people, but still it shook me. It was blood money, but it was my ticket to the good life. In three months, I had gone from sleeping on a slide, to having an apartment, a boat, and over seventy-five thousand dollars. That was the first night all week that I had gotten any bit of sleep.

Jonan sat in his seat chuckling. Samuel was confused.

"What's so funny?" Samuel asked. Jonan just kept on laughing. "Boy, what is so funny?" Jonan stopped laughing and looked up at Samuel.

"This is what you wanted isn't it?" Jonan asked, and then continued laughing.

"What?" Samuel asked.

Jonan stared at his fingers and stopped laughing. "I am about to tell you what happened yesterday," Jonan smiled. "This is the moment that you've been waiting for."

"Well, there is no need to make a show of it. Let's get on with it," Samuel pressed.

"You're telling me not to make a show of it? Me? Officer have you ever heard me tell a story? Making a show out of it is what I do best," Jonan laughed.

"Let me ask you something. You said that your dad is

dead, correct?" Samuel asked.

"Yes."

"I am going to guess that you even made jokes at his funeral. You must've been a riot, weren't you?" Samuel asked.

"You say that like you were there," Jonan answered. "Yes I did. Why do you ask? That's the first time that you've asked me anything other than the story."

"It's because you use humor as a coping mechanism. People do that when traumatic things happen to them. Throughout this entire story you've been making jokes, no matter how bad things got for you. Your girlfriend left you, you made jokes. You lost your job, you made jokes. You were homeless, you made jokes. You nearly died, and yet you still made jokes. You don't need to pretend that none of these things bother you Jonan. It's pretty obvious that you're more sensitive than you try to show," Samuel explained.

Jonan smiled. "You really do have a good read on me don't you?" Jonan asked.

"What can I say? I am good at my job," Samuel answered.

"Or is it because you like me?" Jonan smiled.

"Now you're talking crazy," Samuel answered.

"Oh don't lie. You like me," Jonan laughed.

"Get on with the story please," Samuel demanded. Jonan took a deep breath. He nervously tapped his fingers on the table.

"Here we go."

••

I woke up the next morning and drove to Stewart's Tavern by seven. I was there on time just like I was supposed to be. Natalie picked me up just like she was supposed to. When I got in the car, she greeted me with her typical insult.

"Hey pinhead," She greeted.

I returned with my usual comeback. "Dimwit," I shot back. She drove off. On the drive, Natalie had her typical brand of road rage when a driver in front of us stopped short.

"People with a low enough IQ shouldn't be allowed to drive!" She yelled. "This is why I am pro-choice! I swear!" We continued to talk about nonsense like we had all the time in the world, because it honestly felt like we did.

"So like, do you believe in aliens?" I asked.

"No," Natalie answered.

"Why?"

"Well, we've never proven or disproven it," Natalie answered.

"What if we received a message from aliens. Would you want us to answer it?" I asked.

"Hell no."

"Why not? You said that you don't believe in them?"

"I also don't believe in curses, but I am not going to be looking for the Flying Dutchman's cursed treasure on the off chance that I'm wrong. If there is a chance that I'd get screwed in a way not of this earth, I'd just prefer to sit comfortably in my living room living in blissful ignorance," Natalie answered.

Eventually we swapped cars, just like Natalie and I had done plenty of times before. Then, we got to a desolate location much like we had done plenty of times before. Then, Natalie had to put on my holster because I still couldn't figure out how to do it. Following that, we got out of the car with a briefcase, much like the people in the other car emerged with a briefcase of their own. We did the trade off in a somewhat non-friendly yet professional manner. Then, we headed home. The whole day went on like normal. I had expected the rest of the night to go that way as well.

God damn was I wrong.

It was six o'clock and we were about a twenty-minute drive from Stewart's Tavern. I looked at Natalie, and on a whim, I decided to do something different.

"Natalie, what are you doing tonight?" I asked.

She shrugged her shoulders. "Well, it is a Friday night and I'm in my twenties, so I'll probably spend the night watching movies and cuddling with my cats," Natalie answered.

"Would you want to go back to my apartment?" I asked. Natalie laughed.

"You're crazy," she chuckled.

"No, I mean it. I was thinking that we could go to Blockbuster, and get a Toy Story VHS, take it back to my place, and just hang out all night," I suggested.

Natalie looked concerned. "Kevin, we can't do that," Natalie responded.

"Don't call me Kevin. I hate it when you do that," I snapped.

"What are you going on about?" Natalie asked.

"Natalie, I have a giant, school-boy crush on you, and I want our relationship to extend beyond just being co-workers," I admitted.

"Kevin it's against the rules for us to do that," Natalie replied.

"What is your name?" I asked.

"Natalie," she answered.

"No, no, not that bullshit name. I want to know your real name. Kevin isn't my real name, and I know that Natalie sure as hell isn't yours. I want to know who you are," I continued.

"I am your co-worker Kevin," she responded.

"Tell me who you really are," I pressed.

"Kevin, it is against the rules for me to tell you what my real name is," Natalie explained.

"Well fuck the rules. I want a normal person experience for once. A normal person experience is a relationship, and I want one of those. I want one of those with you," I explained.

"Kevin I-"

"My name is Jonan Casey," I admitted. Natalie slammed on the breaks and put the car in park right in the middle of the road. Thank God there were no other cars on the road so it was okay.

"Get out of the car!" Natalie screamed.

"Natalie I-"

"Get out of the car now Jonan!" She yelled.

"But I-"

"I said now!" She screamed. I opened the car door, and stepped out of the car. "Now close the door!"

"Wait, can I just ask you one thing first," I asked.

"What?" She answered. This was my only chance. I needed to say something to her that would change her mind. I needed to say something to her to make her stay. I needed to convince her to stay there with me. I needed to use all of my brain power to do that.

"Do you think that you're only mad at me because you're on your period?" I asked. That was when she slammed on the gas and the car accelerated away. It went so fast that the door had enough momentum to close. I looked down at my foot. I went to kick a large boulder on the side of the road. "Dammit!" I yelled. When my foot connected with the boulder, it hurt my toes so badly that I hobbled all the way to Stewart's Tavern. It took me about two hours to get back to my car in the parking lot. Then it only took me a few minutes to get home. When I did, I checked my phone. At about six thirty, I had gotten a phone call. There was a voicemail, which I knew could not have been good.

"Kevin, I need to discuss something of importance with you. Anyways, ah, call me back."

There was one person that it could have been; The Dealer. He left his radio on while giving the message, so it was a little difficult to make out what he was saying, but it was clear enough to understand. So at about eight thirty, I called back the number. The Dealer answered the phone almost immediately.

"What on Earth were you thinking?" The Dealer belted.

"I was just-"

"You were just breaking two of the rules that I gave to you! Never give out your real name, and never attempt to advance your relationship with any of your co-workers past a professional one! What part of your brain decided to completely disregard these rules? I cannot believe the impotence, the disrespect, the irresponsibility, and the sheer stupidity that you displayed today!" The Dealer ranted.

"Sir, I'm sorry for-"

"Oh you are definitely going to be sorry boy," the Dealer responded. "Now you listen to me and you listen well. Tomorrow at six a.m. sharp you are going to have a meeting with Lyle in which he will discuss with you re-issuing you a new partner. Is that understood?"

"But what about me and Natalie?" I asked.

"You and Natalie? I'll tell you about you, and Natalie," the Dealer answered. "There is no 'you and Natalie'. You will never see Natalie again nor will you ever attempt to have another meeting with that individual. Is that clear?"

"Sir I-"

"I asked you if that was clear!" The Dealer interrupted.

"Yes, or, no?"

"Yes sir," I begrudgingly agreed.

"Good," he exhaled. "Six a.m. sharp." He hung up.

And that was it. I stood there alone in my apartment holding the phone in my hand. I realized that I fucked up. I broke The Dealer's rules. He told me the previous night just how much trust he had in me, and now I had broken his trust. I lost all of the credibility that this weekend had brought me. The Dealer no longer saw me as a model worker. Now he saw me as a loose cannon. Because of all of that, I was never going to see Natalie again. Just like that, I was alone in the world again. Natalie was the only thing that I liked about the world, and now I had lost her. The thought of that made me want to break down. But then, in the midst of my fit of self-loathing, I had a dark thought.

Lyle.

I was supposed to meet with Lyle to discuss who my next partner was going to be. I had only seen Lyle before at two meetings. One ended in the uprooting of a person's life. The other ended in that person's death. That could only mean one thing. I was Lyle's next target.

The Dealer wanted me dead.

Chapter 16

Jonan sat in silence for a moment. Samuel was watching him. Jonan's face wrinkled and his lips contoured. A bead of sweat dripped off the tip of his nose.

"It was for nothing," he huffed. Jonan sniffled hard. A tear streamed down his face. "It was over nothing. All that I wanted to do was feel like a human being again, not a criminal. Every minute of every waking hour made me feel like a piece of shit, and I wanted something to make me feel normal again. I wanted my old life back. I don't care about the money anymore; I just want a sense of normalcy. I just wanted to have someone in my life. I didn't want to piss off the Dealer, or hurt his sales in any way. Is that too much to ask?"

"So your intentions were not to upset him?" Samuel asked.

"No. My intentions were to have a girlfriend again," Jonan sobbed. "I got cocky because I had gotten on the Dealer's good side. That lasted all of twenty-four hours until I fucked it up! I should have just kept my fucking mouth shut. I didn't want that life anymore! I didn't want to make a living tearing people's lives apart!"

"Well you didn't. You just watched other people tear people's lives apart. You never made that decision. The decision was made for you." Samuel tried to comfort him. Jonan sat back in his seat. His face was beat red, and his eyes were blinking rapidly.

"Well I didn't do anything to stop it," He cried. He sat there quietly again.

Samuel leaned forward. "So what happened next?"

....

Don't move. Don't scream. Don't make a sound.

Mason and Bill had been in my apartment more times than I knew. Therefore, I decided that they must have wired my apartment with recording devices. They were probably listening to my every move. So, I unclenched the phone, and walked to the remote control. I clicked on the television, and blasted it as loud as it could go. I wanted to drown out any noise I made. I did not move quickly, or neurotically. If every sound that I made was being monitored, then it would be easy for them to realize that I was on to them if they heard a lot of banging.

Then I walked to the garbage can. I shifted my hands through all the trash and food scraps. I reached through a week's worth of garbage to find what I was looking for. I clenched it in my hand and gave a little smirk. I removed the advertisement that the car dealership had given to me upon purchasing the used car. It was the flyer for the masquerade party at Stewart's Tavern. It was the flyer with the dumbest gimmick ever. It was set in a way that you could punch out parts of it so that you could turn it into a mask. So that was exactly what I did. I turned the flyer into a mask.

Then I put on my black hoodie, and got my backpack from the bedroom. I walked over to my freezer and took out all the boxes of frozen T.V. dinners that contained all of my money. I also grabbed the shoebox that contained $50,000. I put all of that into my backpack. Within the boxes of T.V. dinners was a grand total of $38,602. That was all of the money I earned over the past three months, all of which was in my backpack now. I made sure to have my car keys in my pocket. Then, I put the hoodie that I wore when working with Natalie in my backpack.

I grabbed the doorknob to my apartment, but before turning it I realized something. Mason and Bill could be in the parking lot. I couldn't leave because they would be right on my tail. They would know that I was on to them. So I needed a new plan. Driving somewhere far away, and starting a new life with nearly ninety grand, was not going to be that easy. I needed to out think them. I needed to do the impossible. I needed to out think the most dangerous men that I had ever met.

The difference between the fear I felt at that moment and the fear I felt over the previous weekend was huge. Over the weekend I was afraid, but knew that I had all of the Dealer's men on my side. But everything had changed. All of the men that were protecting me before wanted me dead now. I was on my own.

I turned away from the front door, and I walked over to a window. I opened it wide and breathed in the night air. I looked down. It was about a two floor drop into some bushes. I sighed.

"Here goes," I exhaled to myself. I climbed up onto the window sill, and fell so that my side landed in the bushes. I heard a crack in my back, but luckily I was able to stand back up. The parking lot was not visible from where I fell, so if Mason and Bill were in the parking lot, they would not have seen my somewhat ungraceful fall. That meant that I was in the clear. I looked around the street for a certain man. There was one person that I needed to find. I searched up and down the street. My heart skipped a beat when I saw the decrepit broken down car.

I exhaled and saw my breath in the cold. I put my hands in my pockets, and pulled the hood over my head. I looked both ways, and casually walked across the street to the most run down car that I could find. I looked inside and saw the man that I needed. There was Randall in the back seat of the car fast asleep. I tapped on the window until I saw him begin to stir. He looked up to see me. He sat up and opened the door. He crawled out of the car and looked at me.

"Jonan, it's so good to see you again man. It's been like, days man. How have you been? How are the kids?" Randall asked. His frame was similar to mine.

"Look, I need you to do me a favor, you understand?" I asked. "It will take all night."

"I don't know man, my schedule for tonight is pretty booked," he answered, scratching his scraggily beard.

"I will give you ten thousand dollars," I argued.

"Well I guess that I can squeeze you in," Randall agreed.

"Does your car run?" I asked.

"Yeah, she works just fine man," Randall answered.

I pulled out my car keys. "Do you want my car?" I

offered.

"To keep?" Randall asked.

"It's all yours buddy, that and ten thousand dollars. I just need you to do me a favor," I elaborated.

"Anything for you man. You're like a brother to me. Not like my real brother though. He's an ass," Randall replied.

I dropped my backpack and removed ten thousand dollars. Also, I removed the flyer mask. "Do you know where Stewart's Tavern is?" I asked. Randall chuckled.

"Of course man, I get trashed there every weekend," Randall laughed.

"Okay good. I need you to wear this mask." I handed him the mask. "Now take my car from the parking lot and go to Stewart's Tavern. They are having a masquerade themed party tonight. Go and have as much fun as you want there. But you need to stay there all night, and wear this mask for the rest of the night, that includes the ride there."

"Okay, anything else?" Randall asked.

"I need to take your car," I answered.

Randall took out his keys. "Okay, so I trade away my mess of a car, party all night, get a better car, and make ten thousand dollars. What is the catch?" He asked.

"No catch," I lied.

Randall handed me his keys. "Sounds like a deal man," Randall laughed. I handed him the keys to my car, the mask, the hoodie that was in my backpack, and the ten thousand dollars. I got into the driver's seat of his car and laid very low so that my eyes could peer through the window without any of my body being visible.

He put on the mask and the hoodie. I watched as a masked Randall walked around the corner of the building. The parking lot was visible from where I was sitting, but I was sure that no one from the parking lot could've seen me cross the street. Randall got into my car and ignited the engine. I watched as he drove to the exit of the parking lot. When he did that, the engine of another car that was sitting in the parking lot turned on. When my car pulled out of the parking lot and turned down the road, the other car in the parking lot drove to the exit of the parking lot. None of its lights were on. I could not tell, but I was sure that that was the car that Mason and Bill were in. They turned in the same direction as Randall, and then they were gone. I could not see them. I sat there for a moment, and a huge smile swept across my face.

But now I needed to figure out what to do. My mind raced. What should my next course of action be? I put my fingers to my temples. My head hurt from thinking so much. What could I use to outsmart the Dealer? What information had he told me that I could use against him? I thought over every single thing that I knew about him. I considered every single conversation that I had had with him. That was when a sentence from one of our conversations struck me.

"I will be meeting with McFowley and Granger at the Pigeon Docks Friday Night to discuss with them what to do about their betrayal."

The Pigeon Dock? I knew where that was! That was the dock that was near the docks where I left my boat. It was almost too perfect. I could go to the Pigeon Dock, kill the

Dealer, and then get to my boat and go to Canada! I would be free! Without their leader, none of them would have incentive to kill me! And even if they wanted to, they would have no way of finding me because I would be in Canada! It was perfect, especially since I never took the gun holster off. Since I had no idea how to put it on, the fact that I never took it off was convenient.

I ignited the engine and it whimpered alive. This automobile was a piece of garbage, but it worked. That was when I began my drive. The drive was not bad. It was only about a half hour. Also, it had begun to rain harshly on the way there. The fact that I was used to drives that lasted hours upon hours made a half hour of driving not seem so bad. The drive felt like it was only a few minutes. Being terrified for your life makes time go by quicker. But throughout the entire drive I kept watching my rearview mirror for anyone who would be following me. Luckily for me, I never noticed the same car in my rearview mirror twice. Nobody was following me. Nobody was hunting me down. Nobody knew where I was, and I had a smile on my face because of it.

I parked in the parking lot of the dock where I left my boat. I left my backpack in the backseat of Randall's car. I looked around and saw no other cars in the parking lot. I guess that everyone else had better things to do on a Friday night than to fear for their lives.

I began walking to the Pigeon Dock. I didn't want a car in their parking lot, screaming of my presence. I needed to make sure that nobody knew I was there. I jogged through the woods in between the two docks. It only took me about a minute to get to the Pigeon Dock. I looked across the wooden docks where all the boats were. There, in the distance, I saw two men in police uniforms. They were standing far out to the edge of the dock. They stood there with another man. I absolutely knew who that man was without a shred of doubt in my mind. Despite the fact that I never met him in person, I knew who he was.

There stood the second evil person that I told you about. There was the devil himself. It was the Dealer in all of his flesh and glory. He stood with his back to me, and he wore a brown overcoat. He also wore a hat on his head, but I couldn't make out the shape of it from the distance. None of the three men were facing my direction, so I sneaked closer to the wooden dock. I hid behind a large boulder that was bigger than my body. The boulder sat at the point that the wood dock met land. I still couldn't make out any physical details of the Dealer, but I could see that his back was to me. Also, the two cops' had their backs to me. The three men were all looking out to Lake Michigan. The cops were closer to the edge of the dock than the Dealer was. He was standing so that the officers' backs were to him. They were clearly talking about something, but I couldn't make out what.

This was it. This was the moment that I had been anticipating. When I went on the kill mission with Lyle, he told me that if you think you are the smartest man in the room, then you've already lost. He told me to always know your enemy's weaknesses. I was pleased to realize that the Dealer had made the fatal mistake that Lyle warned me about. The Dealer assumed that he was smarter than me, and yet I had just gotten two steps ahead of him. The Dealer saw me as an unintelligent child. Well, I just proved him wrong. I had just deceived him. I evaded Mason and Bill. I outsmarted all of them. I showed them what I was truly capable of. I showed them everything that I had, and it felt invigorating. I unclipped my gun from the holster. I clicked the safety off. I peeked my head above the rock, and aimed so that the Dealer's head was right in my pistol's sight. I was about to do it. I was about to kill the devil himself. My finger wrapped around the trigger. I took a deep breath. I heard a loud bang.

But there was a problem. I hesitated. I faltered. And I had not pulled the trigger of my gun. But then where did the bang come from? I looked across the dock to see where the bang came from. With the cops' backs to the Dealer, he shot one of them in the back of the head, causing him to collapse. The other one turned and had his hand on this hip to withdraw his gun. However the last thing he saw was the barrel of the Dealer's gun, and the look of the man who ended his life. The Dealer shot again, the bullet collided with the front of that man's face. Blood spilled onto the front of the Dealer's brown overcoat. The two cops lay on the dock, dead.

Then, a boat much larger than mine came alive. All of the lights turned on and the engine revved. The Dealer jumped onto the back of it, and it sped off into the distance. That was it. I missed my shot. I missed the one opportunity that I had to kill the Dealer. I never even took the shot. I choked. I messed up, and I can admit that.

When their boat was far eough away that I couldn't see it anymore, I stepped out of my hiding place. I took a walk down to the end of the dock. There, in a pool of their own blood, were the two police officers. The rain was washing their blood in between the boards of the dock and into the lake. It was an absolute downpour by then. I just glanced over the cracked skulls of the two men before me. I screamed at the night sky. I wasn't mad at anyone but myself. I had no one but myself to blame for this mess that I had gotten into. My only solution was to go to the boat, and continue with my plan of leaving to go to Canada. I took a step to walk off the dock, but then my worst nightmare came ture.

The flashing red, white, and blue lights. The sirens. I knew what was happening. The cops were there. There they were. Before I knew it, there was a cop car at the end of the dock. Then another, and then another, and then yet another. Cops opened the door of their cars and removed their guns and aimed them at me.

"Freeze!" One yelled.

"Put your hands in the air!" Yelled another. I put the gun back in its holster, and raised my hands in the air.

"No no no no no no no!" I screamed. I needed to get their attention to my words. "This is a complete misunderstanding! If we can just sit and talk, I can work all of this out!"

They didn't care. They just bum-rushed me. I got tackled to the ground and handcuffed. I had my Miranda rights read to me, and I realized that I had fucked up on a whole new level.

Chapter 17

"And there it is. That's my story. The story is over," Jonan finished. "I hope that it was satisfactory to you. If you're friends with David Fincher, you should call him and sell the story to him. I'm sure that they'd eat this shit up."

"You're really cocky you know that?" Samuel asked.

Jonan smiled. "I've been told," He replied.

"So all of that is your official statement?" Samuel asked.

Jonan leaned forward and stared at Samuel. "Every, last, word of it," He answered. "But let me guess; you still think that I'm some dirty cop killer don't you?"

"I just have one question," Samuel began. "All of these dangerous people, if they are as adept as you claim them to be, why are you telling me all of this? That has to be putting you in danger, right?"

Jonan started laughing. "You see, I pondered that all of last night," Jonan began. "Last night the cops were asking me questions, and I refused to answer all them. I thought that if I had answered them, then the Dealer would get somebody to whack me. But then last night, I lay in my cozy prison cell bed, and I thought about how I could get out of this mess. That was when I realized something very important; I won't. I am in too deep. My life is an unrelenting swirling toilet bowl filled with so much shit that it is impossible to flush. I realized that the Dealer made one crucial flaw last night. I realized that I still had one final way of getting him. Lyle actually gave me the idea. On our way back from our kill mission, Lyle told me that he only hits people who have done so many wrong things that they would never go to the police about it. Then, in order to sink Lyle and the Dealer, they would also have to sink themselves. Well, I just happen to be in a very unique position. I sink regardless of whether or not I snitch on the Dealer. If I don't tell my story, I go to prison on two murder charges with the constant fear of one of those prisoners being hired by the Dealer to kill me. On the other hand, if I do speak, I could get lesser charges, and the Dealer would still want me dead. So in this case, speaking out would do more good to me than harm, and that is why I decided to speak." Samuel sat there with him for a moment. Jonan finished by saying "If you think you're the smartest man in the room, then you've already lost."

"So are you still afraid of a police officer working for the Dealer?" Samuel asked.

Jonan sat back in his seat relaxed. "I'm still not entirely sure that you aren't working for him," Jonan answered.

"Well son, I can promise you beyond a reasonable doubt that I do not, and will not work for the Dealer," Samuel answered.

Jonan leaned forward. "Now Officer, I believe that in

your heart you do believe that you have no affiliation with the Dealer, but I think that you have without realizing it," Jonan said.

Samuel turned his head. "How do you figure that?" Samuel asked.

"I believe that some higher up gave you an order, or some higher up gave an order that eventually trickled down to you. That order was somehow influenced by the Dealer. Or maybe you've even met the Dealer himself, and you didn't even realize it. But I don't know, I didn't even get a good enough look at him to positively identify him," Jonan explained.

"I'll be back," Samuel stood up and walked out of the room, closing the door behind him. He rubbed his eyes with his hands and sighed. He walked through the police station to Frank's office. He knocked on the door until Frank opened the door.

"It's so great that you're here because I've been waiting to talk to you," Frank greeted.

"I need to talk first," Samuel answered, closing the door to Frank's office. "Now I might just sound crazy by saying this, but I believe this kid's story. I truly don't believe that it was him who killed McFowley and Granger."

"Well Sam, it is interesting that you say that because we can exonerate him," Frank answered. Samuel took a step back.

"What?" Samuel asked.

"Yup. Remember the mysterious fantasy gun that we couldn't find? We still haven't found it in the water. The kid's gun was proven to not have been fired in weeks, and maybe even months. He never shot a gun before in his life according to his story, and as of now we can't disprove that. Furthermore, the bullets fired at McFowley and Granger don't match the striations that Casey's gun would have given. Also, we found that car that he mentioned in the parking lot of the dock that is next to the Pigeon Dock. His story holds up. So until we find the mystery gun, we have no way of pinpointing who did it. The kid is a criminal, but he isn't a murderer," Frank explained. Samuel leaned his back against the wall with a sigh of relief.

"Thank god. I was afraid that I was going to have to try to convince everyone that Casey was innocent."

Frank chuckled. "Sam it's fine. Of course McFowley and Granger's friends aren't going to be easily convinced, but it's the truth," Frank continued.

Samuel stood up tall. "Jesus today was strange," Samuel sighed.

"No arguments here," Frank agreed. "Also, you want to see something crazy?"

"I think that I have seen enough crazy for one day," Samuel replied.

"Well I'm going to show you anyway," Frank answered. He removed a folder from his desk, and removed large photographs from it. One photograph showed two packages, and the other one showed a piece of notebook paper filled with names and dates that Samuel did not understand. "I found this in McFowley's house. That package contained a kilogram of cocaine, and those names and dates suggest the times that sales occurred."

Samuel looked very closely at the photograph. "So then more of Casey's story holds up?" Samuel asked.

"Yup, and that adds credibility to other aspects of his story. So you can rest easy at night knowing that you helped exonerate an innocent man," Frank continued.

Samuel glared at Frank. "You've got a loose definition of innocent."

Jonan sat in the room by himself for a half hour until Samuel returned.

"What took you so long?" Jonan asked.

"I was looking for what to charge you with, and I went as easy on you as I could," Samuel explained. "You're being charged with selling drugs, which can send you to jail for up to seven years and up to a $25,000 dollar fine. Furthermore, you are being charged with owning an illegal firearm, which carries ninety days and a one hundred dollar fine. Then there is accessory to murder, which can be up to five years, but that one will be way harder to get you with so you may not serve that sentence. I do not know. Optimistically, you are in jail for seven years and ninety days. Best case scenario is that you manage to bring down your punishment even more. I don't see that happening, but you could pull off a miracle."

"Oh good, only seven years of prison," Jonan cheered sarcastically.

"You've got a court hearing tomorrow morning at nine a.m. sharp," Samuel continued, sliding a piece of paper to Jonan. "Your punishment will be decided there, so you are now out of my hands."

"I can't wait," Jonan rolled his eyes.

"Now this is important, and I want you to listen to what I am going to tell you next," Samuel said.

"What is it?" Jonan asked.

"Now, technically I cannot hold you here against your will tonight. So, you can go back to your apartment and sleep in your own bed tonight. However, I would suggest for your own safety to stay in a cell overnight. If you truly believe that these men are going after you, and trying to harm you, then it would be best for you to stay here," Samuel explained.

"Absolutely not," Jonan answered.

"Son, you can stay here. We can protect you. This is in your best interest-"

"Excuse me officer, but I know what my best interests are. I refuse to stay here overnight because out there I am free. Out there I can run from these guys. I can out maneuver them, and I can evade them. I've done it before. Also, if it is my last night of freedom for the next seven years, I am going to milk every last second of it. But in here I'm trapped. In here I am a sitting duck. Let's say that the officer that I'm being protected by just so happens to be alone and enters my cell with a club. Or maybe the security cameras somehow cut out for a few minutes, and by the time they turn back on I am already dead. Or maybe I just so happen to be put in a cell with a prisoner who just so happens to have anger issues, and the next morning I am dead with a swollen neck. I want to put my safety into my own hands. If you want me to make it to that court hearing tomorrow morning, then I need to take my chances," Jonan explained. Samuel raised his arms in defeat.

"You can lead a dumbass to water but you can't make it drink I guess." Samuel unlocked Jonan's handcuffs. Jonan scratched his wrists where the handcuffs had gripped him all day. He stood up and stretched his whole body. "You be careful now son."

"Officer, if I don't make it to the court hearing tomorrow, I need you to know that it will be because I am dead," Jonan explained solemnly.

"So then stay," Samuel pressed.

"Just make me this promise. If I make it to prison, check up on me every three months just to make sure that I'm still alive," Jonan requested.

"I will," Samuel replied.

"You promise?" Jonan asked. Samuel sighed.

"I promise," Samuel answered.

"Is my car outside?" Jonan asked.

"Yeah. The car that you got from Randall is outside for you. We confiscated all of your drug money though," Samuel informed.

Jonan smirked. "Good, my apartment is unsafe to go back to, I traded down to a crappy car, and I have no money for a motel. I guess that I'll just find some slide to sleep on," Jonan joked.

"Do you have any other questions for me?" Samuel asked.

"Yeah, I have one," Jonan grinned. "How did you get that scar on your face?"

"Get out of here," Samuel replied. Jonan chuckled a little. Samuel walked Jonan out of the police station. Many other officers glared at the two as they exited the station. Cops screamed at him. Samuel and Jonan refused to react. They just walked as if none of them were there. The grief stricken officers were not convinced of Jonan's innocence. When they got outside, the sun was gone, and the moon was high in the sky. Samuel handed Jonan the keys to Randall's car.

"Thank you officer."

"I'll go to your court hearing to make sure that you are there," Samuel stated.

"Wish me luck," Jonan requested. He then sprinted to Randall's car. He got in as fast as he could. The engine started, and then he took off. Samuel stood there in the night air. He exhaled, and saw a puff in front of his mouth from the cold. Frank emerged from the station and stood next to Samuel, lighting a cigarette.

"Rough day?" Frank asked, dragging on his cigarette.

"In all my years on this job, I've never heard a story quite like that," Samuel sighed. Frank extended an unlit cigarette to Samuel. Samuel took it in his hand, and Frank lit it for him. Frank exhaled, and let his hands go to his sides.

"You know, when I was your age, I would hear a story and think that I would never hear anything that could top it. Then, I'd be surprised later on with an even more shocking story. You could just put this on your list of crazy shit," Frank advised.

"Well, all I know right now is that I need some sleep,"

Samuel sighed, puffing on his cigarette. Frank blew out smoke.

"Then go," He said, flicking ash off of the end of his cigarette. "Go home to your wife Sam. Get some rest tonight. You've earned it."

"I always think that I am immune to these kinds of stories, but today shook me. I still think that I handle these crazy events better than the average officer, but I'm not perfect," Samuel continued.

"Sam, one day you'll be my age talking to some younger officer, explaining to him some kind of event that made you immune to feeling upset because of the horrible crimes that you see committed. I don't know what the circumstances will be, but by the time you're my age, you'll be better at it than I am now. You're already a better cop than I am," Frank explained. "Now get home. I'm sure that the only person you want to see is Monica."

"Good night Frank," Samuel replied. He walked out to his car, and got in the driver's seat. Samuel drove off with the window down until he finished his cigarette. Of all the interrogations that Samuel had done in his life, this one had to be the most draining. Samuel was exhausted. The previous night he was just sitting in the car with his friend Frank eating fast food. He knew that cops getting hurt was always part of the job, but there was nothing he could have done to prepare himself to witness its effects first hand. By the time that he got home, his cigarette was down to the nub. Samuel pulled into the driveway. He stepped out of the car, dropped his cigarette, and stomped it out. Then, he got back in his car, and pulled it into the garage. The garage door shut behind him. He walked into the house, and heard his wife Monica talking with Uncle Jerry.

"Oh you're home!" Monica greeted, wrapping her arms around Samuel's shoulders.

"Sammy! I'm so glad to see you before I have to leave!" Jerry exclaimed.

"Oh I'm so happy to see you too," Samuel attempted faking a smile.

"I was just saying goodbye to him because his ride is almost here," Monica told Samuel.

"I was afraid that I wasn't going to be able to see you tonight before you left," Samuel told Jerry.

"Me too, but I'm so glad that you managed to get here." Jerry's smile was beaming across his face. "I am all packed and ready to go."

"The driveway looked weird without your car there," Samuel joked.

"I think that a piece of me died when I sold that thing," Jerry laughed.

"Well, I am just glad that you are picking your life up again," Monica stated.

"I am too. I know that I have said this so many times but I'll say it again. I could not have done it without you two. I can't thank you enough." Jerry hugged Monica, and then hugged Samuel.

"Uncle Jerry, it was a pleasure to have you. You could have stayed as long as you wanted, and we wouldn't have minded one bit." Samuel smiled.

"Sam stop saying things," Monica joked. Jerry laughed.

"Oh I wouldn't want to overstay my welcome," Jerry replied. Jerry walked over to the window and looked outside. "Oh my friend's car is outside! I had better get going." Jerry picked up his bags and walked over to the door.

"Call when you get there," Monica requested.

"I will," Jerry answered. "I love you Monica."

"I love you too Uncle Jerry," Monica regarded, hugging Jerry.

"I'll walk you out," Samuel said, opening the door for Jerry. Samuel also carried Jerry's large suitcase. The two stepped outside and shut the door behind them. Their breath was visible in the cool night air.

"Thank you for carrying that suitcase. I can't lift things like I used to," Jerry chuckled.

"No worries. There's no reason that you need to carry this heavy stuff when I'm here," Samuel explained.

"Rough day at work?" Jerry asked.

"You would not believe," Samuel answered.

"Oh I know, trust me," Jerry chuckled.

"Well you've got a lot of hard days of work ahead of you," Samuel replied.

"Oh I can't wait for that. I've got hard work ahead of me for sure," Jerry added.

"Selling vacuums should be fun," Samuel smiled.

"I am definitely thankful for everything that you have done for me Samuel. I know I've said that enough times, but I mean it," Jerry thanked.

"And I know that I have said this enough times, but you were no bother. I enjoyed having you here, honestly," Samuel explained. Jerry opened the door to the back seat of his friend's car. Jerry and Samuel loaded it with Jerry's suitcases. They closed the door, and Jerry opened the door to the passenger seat and sat down. Samuel bent over to look into the window. He saw that Jerry's friend in the driver's seat was a large Asian man. "Call me when you get there."

"I will Sam," Jerry answered.

"Thank you for driving Unc-" Samuel's sentence was cut off by the driver pulling out into the street and driving off into the distance. "-le Jerry for me…" Samuel said to himself. Samuel walked back inside his house to see his wife Monica cleaning dishes.

"So he's gone," Monica smiled.

"Yup," Samuel answered. He sat down at the kitchen table and dropped his car keys on the table. "So you know?"

"Know what?" Monica asked.

"You know about McFowley and Granger?"

"Samuel you're acting strange," Monica replied.

"Jerry told me Monica, you don't have to pretend that you don't know what I am talking about," Samuel said caringly. Monica looked confused.

"Sam, what exactly did Uncle Jerry tell you?" Monica asked.

"Today Uncle Jerry and I went out for lunch, and he told me that you read about the cops getting shot in the newspaper, and that you told him about it. That's what Jerry told me," Samuel answered. Monica still looked puzzled.

"Sam, that never happened," Monica answered.

"What?" Samuel asked.

"Sam, I have never read a newspaper in my life. You should know that," Monica said.

"Oh, so then how did you and Jerry find out about the murders?" Samuel asked.

"You're kidding right? Sam, you told me this morning when you were getting ready for work. Do you not remember this conversation?" Monica asked. Samuel thought back to the morning, and then realized that she was right.

"Oh that completely slipped my mind," Samuel answered. "But then how did Jerry know about it?"

"I don't know, you told me not to tell anyone so I didn't," Monica answered.

"So then how did Jerry know about it?" Samuel asked.

"I don't know. Maybe he heard about it from somebody else. Or maybe he read about it in the newspaper," Monica answered. "Can we not talk about this right now? I'm really tired."

"Alright fine," Samuel answered. Samuel sat in silence for a moment as Monica continued washing dishes.

"So now I guess we can focus on having a baby," Monica smiled.

"Finally," Samuel smiled. It was the best thing that he had heard all day. Monica walked over to Samuel and kissed him.

"We can start tomorrow. I want to go to sleep right now," Monica said.

"The weird thing is that I was about to say that," Samuel chuckled.

"I'm going to bed. You coming?" Monica asked.

"I'll be up in a few minutes," Samuel replied.

"Well if I'm asleep, be quiet.". She started up the stairs. "Love you."

"Love you too," Samuel called back. Samuel sat there in the kitchen digesting his day. He looked over to the library and saw something that surprised him. He stood up and walked towards it. Samuel sat down at the table in the library where he and Jerry had sat the previous night talking. He picked up Jerry's cigars. He realized that Jerry had forgotten them. Samuel smiled and removed one and held it in his hand. "More for me I guess."

He played with it in his hand. Then, he realized that there was weight in both of his pockets. He placed the cigar back on the table, and removed what was in his pockets. In one pocket was his cell phone, which he placed on the table. In the other, was something that he had completely forgot about. It was the tape player that Frank had given him. It had the voice message that the Dealer had left on Jonan Casey's phone. Samuel realized that he had yet to listen to it, so he pressed the play button.

"Kevin, I need to discuss something of importance with you. Anyways, ah, call me back."

It was the Dealer's voice. It was exactly how Jonan described it. All of the words were correct, and he did leave music on in the background of the voicemail. There was something suspicious about the recording that confused Samuel. His eyebrows went cross in confusion. Samuel recognized the recording. There was something strange. He felt like he had heard it before. It was such a strong déjà vu moment. It was such a powerful feeling of familiarity that it could not be coincidence. Samuel had heard this message before, but he could not remember where he had heard it. He listened to the message again.

"Kevin, I need to discuss something of importance with you. Anyways, ah, call me back."

Then he listened to it again.

"Kevin, I need to discuss something of importance with you. Anyways, ah, call me back."

He rewound it slightly.

"Anyways, ah, call me back."

Samuel was stumped. "Where the hell have I heard this before?" He spoke to himself. Samuel's thoughts raced in his head. He thought back to everything that had happened that day, and he could not for the life of him put his finger on it. His eyes drew to his cell phone, which sat on the table next to the cigar. He lifted the phone to his face. He looked at the main menu, and went to his voicemails. He then listened to a voicemail that he had heard the previous night from Uncle

Jerry.

"Hey Sam, it's me. I just wanted to talk to you about something. Anyways, ah, call me back," a voicemail on the phone spoke. Loud music was on in the background. Samuel was perplexed. He instantly thought that it was a strange coincidence. He even chuckled at the thought. He played the voicemail from his phone again. He remembered how Jerry always played loud music when he was on the phone. Samuel remembered how he said that "Master of Puppets" was his favorite song. Then, Samuel played the recording of the Dealer again. He listened to the music in the background this time. It was the same song; "Master of Puppets".

"What the hell?" Samuel whispered in confusion. This coincidence was starting to get even stranger. Samuel remembered that Frank told him that the Dealer's message was received at 6:45 the previous night. Samuel looked at his phone for the time that his message was received. He saw that it read 6:47 the previous night. Samuel was even more confused. He listened to the recordings again and realized that the part of the song perfectly matched what time they were played. Jerry's message had a part of the song that was two minutes after the part that the Dealer had.

Samuel tossed the cell phone and the tape recorder on the table and chuckled. He sat back in the seat with his hands behind his head. "Work is driving me crazy," he sighed. He exhaled deeply. Samuel picked up the cigar from the table and twirled it in his hands. He looked at the coat rack where Jerry's brown overcoat used to be. That was before he said that a man on the bus spilled food on it, which forced him to throw it away. Samuel stopped twirling the cigar and looked at it. He examined the Colombian flag on the side of the Cigar's wrapping. His eyes went wide, and his heart began racing.

"Son of a bitch!" He yelled, chucking the cigar across the room. Samuel sprinted into the kitchen and grabbed his car keys. He opened the door to the garage and jumped into his car. He revved the engine, and clicked the button to open the garage door. As soon as the door was open enough, Samuel slammed on the gas and the car zoomed backwards. The roof of his car clipped the bottom of the garage door on the way out. His car screeched on the pavement. When it reached the bottom of the driveway, he hit a bump and he his tires popped. Then, his car came to a stop. Samuel put his car in park. "What the hell?" He screamed, jumping out of the car. He saw large holes in all of his tires. He looked back to the driveway and saw road spikes at the end of his driveway. His jaw dropped and his eyes went wide.

Then suddenly, a car pulled up in front of Samuel's driveway. The window rolled down, and a muscular Asian man stuck his head out of the window. Samuel faced him.

"Good evening officer Samuel Delcastillo!" He called. "Your wife Monica lives here to my understanding. You guys are trying to have a baby? That's so cute! Now, I would advise you to get back inside, and keep your mouth shut! You'll live a whole lot longer, trust me!"

"Who the hell are you?" Samuel yelled. The window rolled up, and the car began to drive off. The license plate number was covered. "Hey! Get back here!" Samuel began chasing the car on foot. The car outpaced him, and pulled down the street. "Hey!" Samuel screamed. The car continued to get further and further away from him until

Samuel gave up trying to catch it. It was out of his sight. He just stood there in the street defeated.

"Hey!" He called. His yelling got progressively louder with each word. "Hey! Hey! Hey! Hey!"

Chapter 18

The previous night.

"Where is this guy?" Granger asked.

"I told you that he'll be here soon. He told me himself," McFowley answered. Granger had his arms crossed over his chest and was shivering in the pouring rain.

"Well he had better get here quick. I want to get home soon and out of this fucking rain," Granger replied.

"Why are you always so impatient? He told me that he'd be here and he's never lied to me before," McFowley continued.

"I've never met the guy, and you've only met him once. We are meeting in this desolate place where no one can see us. This has to be the sketchiest meeting I've ever had. How do I know that I can trust this guy?" Granger asked.

"Do you not want to make money?" McFowley asked.

Granger shrugged his shoulders. "Alright fine," Granger agreed. Then Granger squinted his eyes at the parking lot. "Hey, I think that someone is on their way over here."

"I told you man," McFowley smiled slyly. Then he whispered. "Now if this thing starts to go wrong, remember your metal buddy on your hip."

"Got it," Granger smiled. "Let's make some fucking money." He chuckled.

The man made his way to McFowley and Granger. He was not a tall man. He was in his fifties, black, had a white beard, wore a brown overcoat, a fedora, and had the craziest eyes Granger had ever seen.

"Lyle?" McFowley asked. "I thought that we were meeting with the Dealer tonight."

"Oh we are," Lyle answered. "But not here. The Dealer has a boat coming for us at any moment. We need to be at the end of the dock for him to pick us up."

"Oh great! Get us out of this God damn rain!" Granger complained.

"After you," Lyle waved his hands for McFowley and Granger to begin down to the end of the dock. The two police officers began walking down the dock with Lyle behind them. They passed by dozens of boats as they walked. McFowley and Granger were further ahead of Lyle, so McFowley began whispering to Granger.

"Something seems sketchy about this to me," McFowley warned.

"Nothing's sketchy about this," Granger whispered back.

"Why are we going out onto a boat?" McFowley whispered.

"To get out of the freezing cold rain. Why else would we?"

"I don't know. Something just seems off about this," McFowley continued. They had gotten ahead of Lyle.

"Would you please wait up for me? I don't move as fast as I used to," Lyle called to them. McFowley and Granger made it to the end of the docks. Lyle was further behind them.

"Weren't you just telling me to trust them?" Granger asked.

"I did say that when I thought we would be talking to the Dealer at the docks. They just changed the plans without telling me. That is sketchy to me," McFowley looked out to the lake water. "I don't even see any boat out there."

"I think that you're-" Granger's sentence was interrupted by a loud bang. McFowley's head burst and he fell to the ground. Granger turned to look behind him to see Lyle holding a pistol with a smoking barrel. Granger reached for the pistol in his holster, but it was too late. The next bullet came from the gun and collided with the tip of Granger's nose, and came out through the back of the skull. Granger fell to the ground next to his partner.

One of the boat's engines revved. All the lights on the boat flicked on. Lyle sprinted to the boat and hopped into it. The boat reversed out of its spot in the dock, and it sped out onto Lake Michigan.

Chapter 19

Jonan's car sped as fast as it could. It went down the back roads of the town. The old engine roared as it continued down the street. Jonan gripped the steering wheel to the point where blisters were forming on his hands. His face was a bright crimson. His breathing was rapid and heavy. Tears were streaming down his face. The car screeched to a stop as it entered the empty parking lot. Jonan jumped out of the car and ran out to the dock. His feet made a clacking sound as they collided with the wood on the dock. He chucked his backpack with a change of clothes onto his boat, and then he jumped on. Jonan scrambled to untie the rope to release the boat from the dock. Turning the key, the boat's engine shuttered, and the propeller began spinning. His boat sped off into the lake.

The wind blew through Jonan's hair. The boat bobbed up and down as it tore through the water. Lake water splashed up at Jonan's face. Jonan looked out to the horizon as he imagined what his new life would be like. He thought of what Canada would be like. He knew that the Canadian citizens had a reputation of being friendly. Also, Canada isn't known for having large amounts of drug gangs. This would be it. It could take a few days to get there by boat, but Jonan was ready for it. Jonan wanted it. Jonan needed it. He had three options; death, thirteen years in prison, or Canada. He realized that there was no option D, so he decided he'd go with option C.

He was nearly drenched in water but he did not care. He wanted to get there as fast as he could. He was freezing, but he had a dry pair of clothes in his backpack. That was all that he had. The police took his money, and his gun. Jonan could not go back to his apartment. That meant that he was homeless, broke, and defenseless all at the same time. His only hope was Canada. He could find a job, get a place to stay, and find a nice girl that he could live with. He just needed to get there.

Then, a boat much larger than Jonan's sped out in front of his boat. Jonan tried to steer away from it, but the side of Jonan's boat hit the side of the larger boat. Jonan fell to the floor. His boat came to a stop. Jonan looked back up at the bigger boat, and saw Mason standing on deck.

"You fucking idiot," Mason laughed. "This dinky little shit is your getaway vehicle?"

"Get out of my way Mason!" Jonan screamed.

"Yeah, I'm sorry but I can't do that," Mason replied.

"I can go to Canada, and you will never have to see me ever again! I will never bother you for as long as you live. You don't even need to know that I exist! Please just let me go!" Jonan yelled.

"Now, the Dealer wouldn't like that. You see, you broke two of his rules. You snitched to the police, and you ditched your meeting with Lyle this morning. So Lyle isn't too happy with you either. Now, what is my incentive to let you go?" Mason asked.

"Your caring personality," Jonan answered.

"Nice try, but I don't have one of those. Guess again," Mason responded.

Jonan took a deep breath. "You know what? I can help you," Jonan stated. "You need me."

Mason began hysterical laughing. "I? Need you? You're out of your fucking mind scumbag! How do you figure that I need you?" Mason laughed. "You must be some kind of God damned comedian."

"You need me because I know something of value to you," Jonan continued.

"Oh please do enlighten me," Mason requested.

"You trust the Dealer, correct?" Jonan asked.

"I'd say so," Mason answered.

"Okay then. I trusted him. McFowley trusted him. Granger trusted him. Arabella trusted him. Where are those people now?" Jonan asked.

"They all got whacked because they pissed off the Dealer! The difference is that I'm not going to do that," Mason replied.

"Oh come on Mason, listen to yourself! The Dealer sees us as disposable! He can get rid of any of us whenever he wants and he doesn't care. Don't you think that he could just as easily turn on you?"

Mason tossed the idea back and forth in his head. "Where are you going with this?" Mason asked.

"You don't need the Dealer!" Jonan continued. Jonan gulped. "You know I had no idea who the Dealer was this whole time. But I think I figured it all out on the car ride here. I know who the Dealer is, and he's been right in front of our faces the whole time. We just didn't see it!"

"Oh?" Mason turned his head in confusion.

"It's Lyle! Lyle is the Dealer! He was there every step of the way. Everything that the Dealer knew, Lyle also knew! Lyle has the same voice as the Dealer! We don't believe that we know what the Dealer looks like, but in reality we've met him multiple times. Open your eyes Mason! Lyle is the Dealer!" Jonan yelled. Mason stared at Jonan for a moment perplexed. He said nothing. "Come on man, say something."

"Well, I don't know. Let's find out." Mason smiled. Mason banged on the door to the inside of his boat multiple times. "Hey Lyle! What do you think?" Mason called. The door opened, and out came Lyle, lighting a cigar with a match. When the cigar was lit, he flicked the match into the lake. Then Lyle took a puff on the cigar, making the front glow a bright crimson. He withdrew the cigar from his mouth, and released a puff of smoke. He stepped over to the rail of the boat and stared at Jonan. His eyes made contact with Jonan's. Jonan's whole body began quivering, not from the cold, but from dread.

"Mason," Lyle began. He slowly tilted his head towards Mason's direction. "What do you think about Kevin's theory?" Mason began chuckling. He looked at Jonan.

"Of course Lyle's the fucking Dealer you moron!" Mason

was laughing hysterically. "What do you think? You think that you're smart? You think that you've cracked the case? You think that you're a few steps ahead of us? Well guess what asshole; you're three steps back and don't have a clue."

Lyle brought his cigar up to his mouth. He inhaled through it, and the end lit up again. Lyle slowly released it from his mouth, and exhaled the smoke.

"Kevin, what would you do if you were me in this situation?" Lyle asked. Jonan trembled. He tried to speak, but he just let out a weak noise. "Kevin, I asked you a question."

"Please let me go," Jonan pleaded. "I can, I can go t-to Canada. I, I can start a new life. You won't ever h-hear from me ever again."

Lyle stared at Jonan. "Now somehow I don't believe that," Lyle replied, keeping his gaze fixed on Jonan.

"You think that I am evil?" Jonan asked. Lyle stood there, not answering. "Someone once told me that if one looks for evil in places where it does not exist, he will trick himself into believing that he has found it. I am not evil. You are looking for evil in me, but it is not there, I can promise you that."

Lyle turned his head, perplexed. "Who told you that?" Lyle asked. Jonan stood there, breathing heavily. He did not answer the question. He just stood there matching Lyle's gaze. Lyle quickly reached his hand underneath his coat and grabbed at his side. Jonan knew what he was doing. Jonan turned so that his back was to Lyle and Mason. He dove for the engine.

"Nnnnnnoooooooooooo-" His scream was cut off by the sound of a gunshot. The bullet collided with the back of Jonan's head, and came out of his face. Jonan's body fell onto the side of his boat. His torso was in the boat, and his arms, shoulders, and head were hanging off the side. His head swung close to the water. His body was limp.

"Oh good, now for the gross part," Mason sighed. He tossed a large rope with a weight at the end onto Jonan's boat. He dragged the boat closer to the side of his boat. Mason then jump from his boat to Jonan's while holding a red gasoline container. Mason dragged Jonan's whole body to the floor of the boat. He then emptied the entire container of gasoline all over Jonan and his boat. "This is going to smell." After the gasoline was distributed all over the boat, Mason tossed the empty container back up onto his boat. Then, he climbed back into it, and stood next to Lyle. "Would you do the honors?"

"Gladly." Lyle withdrew his matchbook from his jacket pocket. He put his cigar in his mouth. Then he took a match from the matchbox. The first scratch did not ignite it, nor did the second. His third strike, however, lit the red end of the match. Lyle stared at the flame for a second, admiring its dancing red glow. Then he flicked it onto Jonan's boat, igniting all of the gasoline.

Mason began clapping. "I love me a good campfire at night! We should have brought marshmallows. I could go for a s'more right about now," Mason proclaimed.

They watched as the flame engulfed the boat. After a while, the flames went out. It had burnt Jonan to a crisp. The boat itself was charred as well. Then Mason lifted a brick from a pile containing a few bricks. He tossed one into

Jonan's boat, splitting it into many pieces. He kept tossing the bricks at the largest sections of Jonan's boat that were left. He did this until he ran out of bricks. The boat was shattered into many pieces, and Jonan's body had split into many pieces as well.

Mason looked at Lyle. "Well, I think that our job is done," Mason smiled.

Lyle stood there, still looking at the water. "Yes, I'd say that we could go now," Lyle agreed. Lyle and Mason walked into the boat to the helm. There, Bill sat at the driver's seat. "Bill, we can leave now." With that, they were off. They drove for some distance. It took them about forty-five minutes to get to where they needed to be. It was a tiny private dock further up north of the Pigeon Dock. It was so tiny that it could maybe fit three boats. However, there were none there. Bill, Lyle, and Mason all got off the boat and onto the dock. They did not bother to secure it. The dock connected to a dirt road. There sat an old brown car. Bill got into the driver's seat, Lyle got into the passenger seat, and Mason got into the back. Mason sat next to someone who had been waiting there for a long while.

"God, I just loved seeing the little shit's head pop like that. Also, what kind of a pussy ass name is Jonan Casey?" Mason exclaimed.

"Stop it Mason," Natalie snapped, staring out the window into the night sky.

Mason looked directly at Natalie. "Oh what's wrong Natalie? Are you mad because we killed your boyfriend?" Mason mocked.

"Mason! I told you to shut up!" Natalie snapped. Mason

began puckering his lips together making kissing noises.

"Mason, leave her alone," Lyle snapped. Then Mason stopped.

"Admittedly, I kind of liked Jonan," Bill revealed in a high pitched squeaky mouse voice.

"Oh Lyle, I almost forgot to tell you about that nephew of yours. He is a smart guy. I swear you were gone for maybe five minutes when his car zoomed out of the garage. That guy caught on fast. He was also built like a truck. I swear. I have muscle, but I would never want to fight a guy like that," Mason informed.

"I must have made a mistake," Lyle replied. "I got sloppy. That's how he caught on."

Bill turned the key to start the engine. "So where are we going?" Mason asked.

"Well the police have to be onto us. We can't go anywhere near Arizona because that is where my nephew thinks I'm going. So…" Lyle reached into his jacket pocket and removed a walkie talkie. He reached it out of the car window. He clicked the button to connect it to a station over and over again very quickly. He did this until the boat that they had been on before erupted in a fiery explosion, sending shards into the lake and fire all over the place. The car then drove off down the dirt road.

"…Where nobody will ever find us."

The End

Author's Note

To everyone who managed to finish, I thank you. To anyone who cared enough to read the author's note, congratulations! You are one of three people who probably did. Speaking of which, hi Mom! Anyway, releasing "The Mysterious Case of the Yellow County Lake", was such a fantastic experience. I had never released a book before, so to hear how everyone supported me was absolutely incredible. My friend Juli was one of the biggest helps in that process. I love writing because I just love great stories. My favorite movies are all movies with deep enriching plotlines that have an ending that blows me away. So that is what I try to do in my writing. One very important thing to do as a writer, or any artist for that matter, is to look at the writing that you do and see what you did wrong. Of course I love compliments, but I needed tough love when it came to my writing. I believe that the only way to improve at anything is to hear something that does hurt your feelings. It hurt a little bit to hear that I did something poorly, but those are things that I need to hear in order to make my writing improve. My first book was such a learning experience. Of course there are a ton of things that I did right in that book, but I am realist and can see what I did wrong. When writing this book, I looked at my first one and wanted to continue doing right what I did right, but change what I think I did wrong. As far as that goes, I think that I accomplished that. "The Mysterious Case of the Yellow County Lake" was a very dark book with few comedic moments. I was in a comedy club for four years performing stand-up routines to crowds and I didn't utilize my comedic talents? I have no clue. For this book, I wanted to be able to swap between being super dark, and being able to laugh. Jonan Casey was my favorite character that I have ever written, because of how diverse of a character he is. We see him

209

be hilarious, and we see him at his lowest. There are scenes that I've seen people read and go into gut busting laughter, and there are scenes that can make someone cry. If I made you laugh, then I accomplished a goal. If I made you cry, then I accomplished a goal. Some scenes were hard to write. Believe me, as an author I was not cold to my characters. That scene where you see the exchange between Lyle and Arabella was without a doubt the hardest scene that I ever wrote, and not just because it was twenty-four pages long and took me five god damn hours straight to write. It was probably more heart wrenching for me than it was for you.

I would like to say thank you. Yes, I am personally thanking you. I put hours upon hours into writing this book. It took me nine months to finish writing the actual story of it, and a few more months working on the title, cover art, ect. Speaking of which, I suck at making titles. That is undeniably the most difficult part of the writing process because it takes me way longer to come up with a title than it takes me to write an entire book. Speaking of things that I suck at, I put the word "for" in random parts of sentences where it doesn't belong. I think that I edited those all out, but if you find any let me know. Fun drinking game, take a shot every time I do that!

Speaking of which, on a final note, I don't want you to see me as some entity that is beyond you. I am a person just like you except that I am probably better looking. Jokes aside, I want you to reach out to me. Tell me your opinions on my books, or just anything about life in general. Here are some contact links:

Email: RichDeZerga@gmail.com

Facebook Page: Richard F. DeZerga

https://www.facebook.com/RichardF.DeZerga/

Twitter: @RichDeZerga

https://twitter.com/

ABOUT THE AUTHOR

Richard DeZerga Published this book at age 18, however writing had been a passion of his throughout his whole life. He started professionally writing at age 17 when he published his first novel, "The Mysterious Case Of The Yellow County Lake". Other things that Richard is Passionate about are music and movies. Some of his favorite movies include Fight Club, Se7en, Primal Fear, Deadpool, Pulp Fiction, and most importantly, The Usual Suspects. Some music artists that he listens to are Metallica, Twenty One Pilots, Red Hot Chili Peppers, Radiohead, and Phil Collins. Also, Richard plays guitar. Richard grew up in Freehold New Jersey with his mother Kathleen, his father Richard, and his sister Christine. He attended Freehold Township High School, and Ramapo College of New Jersey.

LUNA PHOTOGRAPHY

"Life's Moments In Still Frames!"

Angelica Pasquali is the photographer for Luna Photography. Her passion for photography have been developing and maturing over the years; educating herself throughout high school and college with countless hours of self-exploration of the art. Photography has the power to relay a message to its audience with visuals. Her focus is on creating photographs that have an impact no matter the subject. She has worked with a wide range of events, including: weddings, concerts, sports, authors, models, and more. It is always constructive challenge to push oneself out of their comfort zone and explore different reigns of their passion, which she continues to do.

She has won several awards on regional levels and has made many accomplishments so far as a young photographer. She has won a *Gold Key*, three *Silver Keys*, and three *Honorable Mentions* from the Northern NJ Regional Scholastics Art and Writing Awards. In achieving the aforementioned awards her work was judged by a jury of professional artists, curators, and arts educators. These educators spent 30+ hours reviewing over 3,700 works of art submitted by over 1,100 individual student artists from across northern New Jersey. Her work was selected as part of the top 7% in the region to have been awarded the *Gold Key* particularly. Her works have also been published in *Steppin' Out Magazine*! As her work accomplishments grow, the biggest accomplishment is being acknowledged and appreciated as a true artist in the field.

lunaphotographyap.wix.com/luna

lunaphotography.ap@gmail.com

Other Work Available on Amazon:

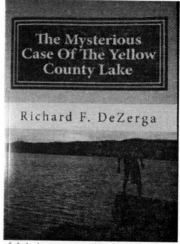

The Fourth of July is supposed to be a fun day of American celebration. However, this year it took a turn for the mysterious. "Yellow County" had a reputation for being a small boring community where nothing exciting ever happened. However, in the days following a Fourth of July celebration gone wrong, the mysterious death of a local teenager became front page news. With the police taking too long with the investigation, the friends of the dead teenager took it upon themselves to do some investigating of their own. Every detail that emerged only brought more questions than answers. Meanwhile, every one of their friends dealt with their grief differently. Experience with these characters the shift that takes place within their minds and their actions, as they try to understand how their friend met his end. Watch as every character develops differently, and has something completely new to add to this unique and gripping story.
"The Mysterious Case of the Yellow County Lake" will keep you guessing with every page, until the jaw dropping conclusion that you will never forget.